Smith
Smith, Travis Ian
Indie darling

$16.00
ocn949889996

Feather Imprint Paperback e

Indie Darling

D1430719

Indie Darling

Travis Ian Smith

2016 A Feather Imprint Paperback Edition

Published in the United States by

a feather imprint
638 Julia Street
New Orleans, LA 70130, USA

Cover design: Narciso Chavez

First Edition

Indie Darling / by Travis Ian Smith
Library of Congress Control Number: 2015956739

Printed in the United States of America

www.travisiansmith.com

ISBN-13: 9780692571590
ISBN-10: 0692571590

for David, my backbeat

for Krystall, my heartbeat

There's a guy in my block, he lives for rock
He plays records day and night
And when he feels down he puts some rock 'n' roll on
And it makes him feel alright
And when he feels the world is closing in
He turns his stereo way up high

Look at me, look at you
You say we've got nothing left to prove
The King is done, rock is done
You might be through but I've just begun
I don't know, I feel free and I won't let go
Before you go, there's something you ought to know

–Ray Davies, The Kinks, from "A Rock 'N' Roll Fantasy"

Indie Darling

Track One

At the start of Winter Break last year, three days of freezing rain shut down the entire city of New Orleans. For the first time in months, I felt released. I opened a bottle of wine, caught up on some reading, and settled in. My loneliness fit me like a favorite pair of socks.

Then I got a call from Tom, my old drummer.

"Have they come to you?" he asked.

In his breathy panic, I didn't recognize his voice.

"Who is this?"

"Tom, shithead."

"What are you talking about?"

"Rudy Silverman just left my house."

My stomach sank from the imaginary fall. Rudy Silverman is the host of *Bands Back Together*, a reality TV show that tracks down the members of a once-famous band to persuade them to reunite for a single televised concert. His surprise visit to Tom's apartment in Seattle meant that our old band The Vows had been selected for the show.

"What did you tell him?" I asked.

"Am I on speaker or something?" he questioned.

"What did you tell him?" I repeated louder, having already lost my patience, which normally took about two minutes with Tom, so we were right on schedule.

"That I'd play the gig if everyone else wanted to."

I laughed him off, remembering all the times I had fallen for one of Tom's bullshit pranks. Maybe time hadn't changed him at all, I wondered. Maybe Tom was still the nervous, dreadlocked, weed-loving jester I always knew—the nerdy weirdo who could smack his drums louder than anyone. I could easily imagine him, high as Pluto in his dark apartment, telling me this concocted story so he could laugh his ass off until he had to stop from coughing.

"Seriously, they just left," he said. "Ask Theresa."

I could hear Theresa, his wife, corroborating his story in the background. I hadn't heard her tinny, falsetto voice in years.

Because Tom didn't have cable, I had to explain to him how *Bands Back Together* worked and what we might expect. Then, just to mess with him, I told him that most bands don't actually play the reunion gig at the end of the episode; they just bitch and sulk the whole time, proclaiming they would rather pump gasoline into their assholes than be on the same stage again with their old band mates. *Bands Back Together* starred the venom of washed-up, vengeful, middle-aged musicians every Thursday night at 9pm, so I rarely missed an episode. "Did he say when he's coming to New Orleans?" I asked him, still not completely sure that he wasn't messing with me.

"Who's going to New Orleans?"

"Rudy Silverman, ass idiot." Whenever Tom and I spoke, we resorted back to using the immature lingo of our former selves—how we spoke to each other when The Vows was at its zenith.

"I couldn't really concentrate with all those cameras in my face," he said.

"So you don't know when this is all supposed to happen?"

"Not really. Weeks? Maybe days? I don't know. Fuck."

"Tom, if you're lying to me—"

"Dude, I'm not. Chill."

Even though I hadn't seen Tom in years, I knew he was pacing in wide circles as he spoke those words to me, nervously pulling his dreadlocks down over his eyes for continuous, useless inspection. There were seven or eight things about him, gestures that he would do, that I could imitate from memory, forever. Being in a band with someone for as long as I was with Tom, traveling up and down every highway from Austin to San Francisco to Minneapolis, sharing the same mangled toothbrush, arguing over set lists, stealing each other's bed, waiting around backstage, trying to make out with the same girl, whatever, is like being in a submarine with someone, down below, at sea, for years. You get to know a person. And among the guys in the band, I got along best with Tom. But he could press my buttons faster than a mischievous kid in a hotel elevator.

"Okay. I'm just saying," I said, lowering my voice, deciding to trust him.

Then it sounded like he was trying to eat the phone because there was so much static on the line. "Look," he said, fumbling some papers in the background, "I had to sign some kind of contract. I can go down to Kinko's right now and fax this shit to you if you don't believe me."

"No, it's cool."

"Alright, then. Don't eat my Viagra."

"What?" I asked skeptically, forgetting Tom's habit of trying to coin stupid, catchy catchphrases. Tom was, I swear, the first person to ever say the word *chillax*.

"I said don't eat my Viagra," he repeated confidently.

"Sure, whatever."

"Don't fart in my refrigerator."

"Thanks. Got it."

While Tom kept babbling, I went over all the possible scenarios in my head. I knew that Mike, our bassist, was back in Austin, working at a bike shop. And the last I heard of Gary Davis Gary, our world-famous lead singer, was that he was living in L.A., trying to put together a new band, Dharma Slums, or something like that. In fact, one of my students had recently brought me a photograph of him in a magazine, and I was pleased to see that he looked about ten pounds heavier. *Happiness is a warm gun.*

"Hello, paging Noah Seymour. Come in, Noah Seymour."

"What?" I answered, annoyed.

"What do you mean *what?* Talk to me, buddy," Tom protested. "This is not the time for you to slip into one of your voids."

I told him what I had been thinking—that since Rudy Silverman interviewed Tom first in Seattle, I figured that he would most likely work his way east, interviewing Gary next in L.A., and then Mike in Austin before he got to me in New Orleans. But *Bands Back Together* was known for ambushing band members in the most unlikeliest of places—as they clocked in for work at six a.m., or as they circumnavigated a forlorn parking lot in Anytown, USA, beleaguered by grocery bags and screaming kids, so I knew that Rudy Silverman could show up anytime, anywhere. I just hoped it wasn't when I was teaching. I knew my administration wouldn't look too kindly on that.

"Will you play the reunion show or not?" Tom finally asked, having summoned the courage to lift the heavy thing weighing on his mind, his voice barely audible at the end of his question, out of nervousness. He knew my wound was deep.

"I bet you called Gary before you called me," I replied, ignoring his question. I almost felt bad for him.

"Come on, Noah. Theresa and I need the money. We live in a dump, bro. It's like Iraq here, up in this shit. Shock and awe, man. Shock and *fucking* awe."

"I'll think about it."

"Don't be a dick. Let bygones be bygones."

"I'm not being a dick."

"Yes, you are."

Click. And I hung up on his ass.

Yet despite my feigned indifference on the phone that day, I knew that Tom's call represented the second chance I needed. Metaphorically speaking, my life had been on pause for too long. It was time for someone to press *play* again.

Track Two

I was once famous. That's the hardest thing for me to say about my life.

I was once famous.

Gary, Tom, Mike, and I made a little noise, got signed, recorded an album, started touring (I fell in love), and then *boom*. They shot and betrayed me, threw my ass into a river. I was kicked out of the band that I—more than anyone else—made famous.

Then people began to recognize me for what I no longer did. Strangers would approach me at record stores or at the bank and ask, "Hey, aren't you that guy in The Vows? Don't you play guitar? Is it really you? It can't be you."

I said yeah, yeah. *Except I don't do those things anymore*, I told myself.

I used to. I used to be. I used to be happy.

A few months prior to Tom's phone call to me about *Bands Back Together*, I was flipping through channels when I saw Brian Finnegan, the once-famous child actor, now all grown up and grey-flecked, living the bizarre-yet-happy life in sunny Los Angeles, the new star of a reality TV show. The viewer is supposed to take pleasure in watching Brian do the normal, applauseless things of everyday life—he picks up his dry cleaning, negotiates his way out of unfair parking tickets, gets his chest waxed, falls in love with a complicated girl, etc. Except I saw something in Brian Finnegan that perhaps most don't see. I saw just beneath his smiling, *isn't-my-life-is-so-great* countenance a quiet turmoil, a hidden sadness that I recognized all too well. I turned off the TV and made my decision. I needed a new start. I needed to shake the Brian Finnegan Disease.

So I became a high school teacher.

Teaching, I knew, would give me summers off and the steady paycheck I needed, but it also meant that I would have to spend the majority of my days with acne-infested, hormonally whacked adolescents. *Not immediately radical*, I thought to myself, channeling one of Tom's memorable catchphrases, but I needed a job, maybe a new career, something, so I watched every high school movie I could get my hands on and reasoned that maybe my rock-n-roll past would score me some points with the kids.

On my first day at Randolph Academy, however, I was a total dick and shot as many evil glares at my students that I could get away with without breaking my newfound persona. I was following the stern and sage advice given to me by nearly every veteran teacher—*Don't smile until Christmas.* Start off strict, they said, and then gradually loosen your noose. If I failed to establish my authority in the first few weeks, they forewarned, I would suffer prolonged, unavoidable, and miserable chaos until the end of the year.

But my students were quiet, docile, *boring* even. I reasoned that maybe my dickhead approach had turned the kids against me, so I began telling lame jokes to lighten the mood. Little did I know that my students were only readying themselves for a full-fledged attack. It happened a week later, during the final period that Friday. Five minutes before the bell rang, Jesse Butler's hand went up into the air like a warning shot. The class fell silent. I should've known.

"Jesse?" I asked, smiling.

"Mr. Seymour, uh, did you get a lot of ass when you were on tour?"

I was stunned. "That's inappropriate. See me after class."

Then Marc Mucha's hand shot up, causing another round of muffled laughter.

"Can you score us some beer for the weekend?"

"Both of you, see me after class," I responded weakly, suddenly aware that I should be nestled back at my house, listening to my records and plotting my revenge against Gary, Tom, and Mike. My students weren't sweet and innocent; they were infidels, heretics, and villains with braces. Word must've gotten out that I was in The Vows because I hadn't told anyone yet. For the last few minutes of that class, every time I asked a student a question, they would only answer by using lyrics from Vows' songs. "Miss Meehan," I remember asking poignantly, "what exactly is Hemmingway trying to express in 'Indian Camp'?"

"I lit the stars in your eyes and never looked away," she joked, smiling.

"Class, I'm serious. Settle down," I begged. "Can anyone tell me the difference between a simile and a metaphor?"

"You're too abstract, girl, like the name of a star I can't remember," David Patterson responded.

They were right. I did write a lot about stars.

At home one night, I drafted a simple resignation letter but decided that I should at least finish the semester. After the close of the first quarter, I threatened endless detentions and grade failures, and things simmered down for a week until Steve Walker's cell phone went off in the middle of a *The Catcher in the Rye* test with "She Is So Deep," our highest charting song, as its ring tone. A week later, I caught Greg Smalley passing around an old copy of *SPIN*, opened to a photograph of me playing my guitar with three cigarettes in my mouth (Agnes, my ex, dared me to do that one night in Seattle to make fun of a popular guitarist at the time). Then, on the day I was being evaluated by my department head, Tommy Moreno thought it would be *hilarious* to bring his acoustic guitar to class, and I swear to God that it took everything I had not to shatter his piece-of-shit Epiphone in front of everyone like a true punk rocker. My life had gone from playing sold-out shows in Brooklyn to coveting things like paper clips, Taco Tuesdays, and copy machines. My fall from grace was absolute.

Yet despite my abject failure as a teacher, I had, ironically, become a celebrity on campus. It was difficult traveling in the hallways without getting random high-fives from students I didn't even teach. To seek refuge, I often ate my lunches,

alone, in the faculty parking lot, with my headphones on, trying to drown out the day's failures by listening to my playlists.
There wasn't a single colleague of mine, as far as I could tell,
who didn't want me fired. *I can't wait to see his stylish ass get
canned*, I overheard one notoriously bitchy Spanish teacher
say as I walked past the faculty lounge one afternoon, head
down, pretending to read my handouts on *Of Mice and Men*.

One student made a remarkable impression on me
because he was always within sight, like a peripheral blur in
my field of vision, a cataract. He was difficult to miss because
of his red hoodie, which he wore always, hood up, his head
covered like a boxer—a male, hipster Little Red Riding Hood
striding across campus. He wasn't one of my students, so I
nicknamed him Weebly, although I later learned his name
was Miles.

When I was fairly confident that the little fucker was, in
fact, stalking me, I asked Chloe Sorensen, the school's young
guidance counselor, about him one morning in the copy
room. Chloe spoke of him fondly and asked me if I could
keep my eye on "the poor fellow" (I hadn't told her yet as to
why that wouldn't be difficult). Apparently, Miles was the darling of the Guidance Department, as well as the grandson of
Claude "Clover" Lafayette—the legendary, populist governor
of Louisiana who once survived a near-death poisoning while
in office. Chloe confided in me that she was in the process of
evaluating Miles because of a screenplay he wrote in Creative
Writing about an adolescent depressive who kept driving his
car off the Mississippi River Bridge.

"So we have a screenwriter here at Randolph?" I asked nonchalantly, although I was a little intrigued. My stalker was a little Quentin Tarantino.

"Yes, and a pretty good one. I think he plays music too."

"Hum," I said. I was a real talker.

"Call me Chloe, by the way," she said, extending her hand out to me. "I'm a big fan of The Vows."

"Oh, yeah?" I answered. "That was a long time ago."

"My boyfriend and I used to make out to *The Weary Boys* in college. Any chance of you guys getting back together?"

At that point in the year, I had yet to receive Tom's phone call about *Bands Back Together*, so I wasn't lying when I told her *no, sorry, not going to happen.*

"Why? Do you and your boyfriend need another album to make out to?" I asked her, trying to change the subject.

"Please. I would need a new boyfriend first."

I had a hard time believing that Chloe was single. Tall, blonde, and athletic—she was, according to the window stall in the boys' bathroom at Randolph, *the holy deliverer of wet dreams* at that mostly sexless, flaccid school. Whenever she ventured from her office and graced us with her presence in the hallways, most boys would stop and stare, stunned for a moment like bees subdued by smoke. Personally speaking, she reminded me of one of those wholesome girl-next-door actresses who play kind-hearted doctors on primetime television. She wasn't my type exactly, but she was flirting with me.

"What happened to your man, your boyfriend from college?" I continued, shuffling my quizzes on dependent clauses for the third time. I didn't want to make it obvious that I was lingering in the copy room just to talk to her.

"Yeah. Steve. Unemployable blogger now. Hopeless."

"Aren't they all?" I replied.

"And you, Noah," she asked, "are you dating anyone?"

"God, no. I'm drowning here. I wouldn't have time for it."

"I heard," she said.

"Heard what?"

"That you're drowning. Here. At Randolph. Sorry."

Then we shared a moment of silence together like a piece of cake. I blushed, taciturn.

"Well, keep in touch," she finally offered, reaching out to shake my hand for the second time. "And befriend Miles, if you can. He needs someone like you to mentor him."

I'd like to mentor that ass, I said to myself as I watched her walk down the hallway in the direction of her office.

Later that afternoon, as I performed my required duty of patrolling the chapel steps during the second half of lunch, I confronted Weebly, a.k.a. Miles, who was sitting a few feet away from me, as always, his hand inside his second bag of Cheetos, his head buried inside a well-thumbed copy of *The Catcher in the Rye*. At least the kid had decent literary taste.

"How's that page you're reading, bub?" I asked, deciding to take a hardline stance against him. It was like a good cop/ bad cop routine except there was no good cop around.

"Excuse me?" he replied innocently, looking up and shielding his eyes from the sun. Without the red hoodie concealing the sides of his face, I finally got a good look at him—cropped strawberry-blonde hair with a spiraled cowlick at his hairline, untrustworthy hazel eyes, and an endless constellation of freckles across his slightly cherubic face. Miles was a ginger. My eyes fell to his backpack cluttered with small decorative buttons championing rock bands from the last thirty years. *Cheap Trick. The Beatles. R.E.M. Arcade Fire. Camper Van Beethoven.* I couldn't find a Vows button, though.

"It's Miles, right?" I asked. "You're stalking me, kid."

He dropped a Cheeto to the ground, picked it back up. "Do you teach here or something?" he asked.

"That's bullshit and you know it."

We were both taken aback, momentarily, by my cursing. Then he bowed under the pressure. "I'm a huge fan of The Vows, you know."

"So you *are* stalking me."

"You're Noah Seymour," he replied, "one of the best guitarists of the past twenty years." His words were flattering, but I brushed them aside.

"You're giving me the creeps."

"I'm not gay or anything."

I had already figured as much.

"Why don't you hang out with your friends?" I asked him.

"Kurt, Jimi, and Tennessee are kind of dead right now."

"Right," I said faintly, not ready for his sense of humor.

"Why are you here?" he asked me. Except he uttered his question very slowly, one word at a time, so that it was clear what he thought of my new profession. For a moment

I considered telling him about the Brian Finnegan Disease, but I didn't want to open up to the kid. Instead, I lied to him, saying that I *liked* teaching.

"This place is death," he answered immediately, his cherubic face completely serious.

"Hmmm, high school as graveyard. Profound."

Then the bell for fifth period rang and he flipped his red hood to cover his head. "Why don't you start another band?" he asked me, grabbing his backpack.

"Kurt, John, and Jimi are kind of dead right now," I told him.

"Ha. Funny."

Soon my lunchtime conversations with Miles became an afternoon regularity, as I was chained to the chapel steps during the second half of lunch and he knew where to find me. It turned out, though, that Miles was quite a Vows fan after all, as he would bombard me with endless questions about certain events in the band's history, some of which I couldn't even remember. I tried to make it very clear that he thought way too much about my former life. "Are you trying to write my freaking biography here, kid?" I would ask him often. To which he always replied, "No, the ending would be too depressing," meaning that I had become *a high school teacher.*

When I saw Miles on the last day before Winter Break, alone and hunched over the liner notes of my favorite Spoon album, *Girls Can Tell,* I passed him in the hallway without speaking. Later that afternoon when I told Chloe that Miles and I had gotten into the habit of speaking to each other at lunch, she seemed impressed. "Any big plans for the holidays?" I asked her in the school's parking lot, where I was ready to fly the fuck out of that place. Chloe was rocking her sexy-librarian look that day, I remember, wearing a tight skirt, nerdy eyeglasses, and a white blouse that revealed a little too much cleavage for a high school campus. *You're an unplanned pregnancy just waiting to happen*, I thought, remembering another one of Tom's catchphrases.

"I'm going to Tennessee for a few days around Christmas and then I'll be back here, you know, just sort of hanging out," she replied. She was making it obvious.

"When you get back, would you like to go fuck each other's brains out?"

Except I didn't really ask her that.

"I know it's unheard of in this city, Chloe," I stammered, "but would you like to, um, go out on a date with me when you return?" It took way too long for my question to come out. But she smiled, answering, "That sounds nice, Noah. But only if you treat me as a perfect gentleman would and have me back home by eight-thirty."

"Agreed. No funny business here."

After an awkward side-hug, she walked away towards her tiny black Mercedes—all beeping and flashing because she had just pressed her remote-key thingy—only to glance back at me after a few steps, to see if I was still watching her. I knew that I was going to have to get my shit together if I was going to sleep with her.

I was happy when she called me a week later, on Christmas Eve, from her relative's house in Memphis. With all the bad holiday music blaring in the background (I think it was Elvis in C minor), I imagined her in a tight, tacky, woolen green-and-red Christmas sweater with a glass of eggnog in her hand. I, on the other hand, was spending the holidays alone.

"Merry Christmas, Noah!" she exclaimed loudly, her voice triumphant over the rattle of her relative's house. "What's going on? Are you in the holiday spirit?"

I had just received Tom's call about *Bands Back Together*, so I was excited to tell her that I might be on network television in a few weeks. I knew that reuniting with The Vows wouldn't hurt my chance of sleeping with her. I'm not *that* dumb.

"That's awesome. Wow," Chloe answered, sounding fairly tipsy. "Congrats. *Holy shit.*"

"Have you ever seen *Bands Back Together?*"

"It's one of my guilty pleasures, yes. I watch it from time to time."

"Will you and your boyfriend get back together and make out if we play the show?" I asked her, trying to flirt. I wasn't sure that she'd be able to hear me with all the noise in her background.

"I don't know. He's right here. Let me ask him."

"Ha-ha. Funny, Chloe."

Then she made me promise that I'd tell her, when she got back, why The Vows broke up in the first place. Before I drifted off to sleep that night, I watched three episodes of *Bands Back Together* with the intensity of a professional quarterback analyzing film before a big game. In the last epi-sode they aired that night, the band Cactus Flower pulled the plug on their reunion gig five minutes before they were about to take the stage—*over creative differences,* they said. But I think it had more to do with the fact that the lead singer found out that the guitarist had been fucking his wife for years. Such a familiar story. I swear the rancor between band members is unparalled.

Track Three

It happened exactly how I feared. On a school day. At Randolph Academy. First period. *Fuck.*

I saw Rudy Silverman, the host of *Bands Back Together*, lingering in the hallway, peering in through my classroom window. I waved him in, accepting the inevitable, like a criminal finally discovered in his hideout. He walked in briskly with a film crew of maybe three or four guys. In no time, bright lights blasted across my face. I didn't even have time to straighten my tie or fix my hair. "This is Rudy Silverman from *Bands Back Together*," he said in his suave, made-for-television voice. "I'm standing next to Noah Seymour, the lead guitarist and songwriter for The Vows, who's now a high school teacher in New Orleans. What Noah doesn't know is that in the past three weeks every other member of The Vows has agreed to reunite for a televised concert to be filmed, next month, at a place of their choosing."

My students were staring at me, stunned.

"So, Noah, what do you say?" Rudy continued. "Will you agree to play a televised show with your former band mates to please your legion of fans?"

I think one of my students said *Holy fuck* out loud, but no one paid him any attention.

"Do it, Mr. Seymour," I heard Gordon Schmidt say from the back corner, where he had been banished for being eternally disruptive. "Don't be a pussy," he continued.

I took a breath and smiled. "Yes, I'll do it," I said. "I'll play the show."

Tevin Do stood on top of his desk and did a spot-on Pete Townsend impression, striking his imaginary guitar over and over again in a grand windmill fashion. "Mr. Seymour gonna be on TV! Mr. Seymour gonna be a rock star again!" he yelled out proudly.

My classroom erupted into chaos.

By fourth period, I found myself in the headmaster's office getting an earful from the administration. Randolph Academy isn't the kind of place that prides itself on having RSTV camera crews invade its tranquil campus, creating a frenzied spirit of rebellion and anarchy among its student body. The administration tends to value *honor, intellect,* and *truth* over disruption and rock-n-roll sabotage. To smooth things over, I pretended that I had no idea that *Bands Back Together* even existed and promised them that it would never happen again. After a ten-minute lecture from Assistant Principal Dick Knowles about choosing academics over "be-bop," I was free to go back to my classes, but Mr. Perriloux, the school's headmaster, asked me to return the following morning during my off period.

Frail yet dignified in his old age, and whiskered like a catfish, Mr. Perriloux was the calm, noble rudder upon which

Randolph Academy sailed through its sometimes-turbulent history. Known for his hunger for racial equality, he fought to guarantee that every student who qualified for admission at Randolph would be accepted, regardless of race or economic status—a victory that ensured that the student body at the most exclusive prep school in New Orleans would be as diverse as the city's population itself. Personally speaking, I also liked Mr. Perriloux because he seemed to favor me for some reason. I later learned that such was his universal appeal—he made everyone who came into contact with him feel valued and special.

When I sat down in his office the next morning, alone, with the door closed, he put me at ease right away. "I'm sorry that you had to suffer through that grand inquisition yesterday. Between you and me, what you saw was a lot of political posturing for someone else's future gain."

"I felt like Hester Prynne in here, half-expecting to be handed a scarlet letter to wear or something."

"You didn't bear the illegitimate child of the town's minister, did you?"

"No, sir, I didn't," I said, laughing. "I guess you're right."

Then he shuffled some papers on his desk and rubbed his long mustache.

"Noah, we haven't had much chance to talk this year. Sometimes at Randolph, as you probably know by now, we're not afforded the luxury of having a lot of time to foster personal relationships among the faculty."

"Yes, I agree, sir."

"So I just wanted to take a moment this morning to find out how things have been going for you this year."

"Good. No complaints. Certainly challenging."

I was speaking mostly in phrases rather than clauses, I knew.

"And you are enjoying teaching your classes, I presume?" he asked, offering me a slender piece of carrot that he had taken from a bag on his desk. Mr. Perriloux was so slim and diminutive in his old age that people joked that he had to eat constantly in order to defend himself against death. "Is teaching what you thought it would be?" he asked.

"It's harder than I thought, but that's what makes it interesting, I guess."

His eyes told me that he needed more from me. He wasn't going to let me off the hook so easily. "Well, I'm having trouble keeping my classes under control, but I'm learning," I answered him, hoping those words would suffice.

"Yes, our young Randolph misanthropes have been historically tough on new teachers. You're not the first, or the last, I promise you."

I didn't say anything.

"Because I'm afforded a little dignity in my old age," he continued, "I'll spare you my own horror stories of being a rookie teacher, but you have to be firm and set high expectations for your students. Don't give an inch to the students who seek to distract you from your true purpose here, which is to shape and educate young souls so that they will be prepared academically and emotionally for the world."

Then Mrs. Spaulding, Mr. Perriloux's secretary, knocked on the door. After she poked her head in, apologized, and smiled at me, she told Mr. Perriloux that his next appointment was waiting for him.

"Please tell him to wait, will you? I'd like to speak to Mr. Seymour a little bit more," he said, pointing in my direction. When she closed the door behind her, he cut to the chase, as they say. "What was all that ruckus yesterday, Noah? We're not used to that kind of commotion around here."

"Well, again, sir, I'm sorry about all that. It was a film crew from a television show."

"A television show?" He was more anxious than impressed, I could tell. He got up from his chair and began feeding his fish.

"Yes, sir. A television show that attempts to get broken-up bands to reunite for a televised concert?"

"I take it that you played music in a band before? You were some kind of musician?" he asked, while making cooing sounds at his goldfish and lightly tapping their tank.

"I played guitar in The Vows?" I asked stupidly, thinking that perhaps Mr. Perriloux had heard of us, as though he might be Gary Davis Gary's most ardent fan or something.

"And you were quite successful at it, I understand?" he asked. "I presume they don't ask just anyone to appear on television, right?"

"Yes, sir. About nine years ago, we toured around the country quite a bit."

When that didn't seem to impart to him the scope of our success, I told him that *The Weary Boys* had been nominated for a Grammy for Best Alternative Album. Still, from him, nothing; he wasn't impressed.

"Okay," he finally said, nodding. "I see. And is this what you want? Another shot in the music business?"

"Well, that's a difficult question to answer." I didn't feel like lying to him.

"Why is that?"

"Well, you're my boss, sir. It's hard for me to speak openly about it, especially when you're asking me if I would choose a career different from the one you hired me for."

"I appreciate your honesty, Noah. But I'm not asking you these questions as your employer. What do your parents think of all this?"

"Both my parents have passed, sir," I said. I'm sure I had told him this, a few times, before.

"Oh, I'm sorry to hear that."

"Thank you. My mother died when I was quite young, and my father died around ten years ago. In Galveston."

"Oh, that's right. You're not from New Orleans," Mr. Perriloux said, disgruntled by his poor memory. "Do you have any other family here in New Orleans?"

"No, just me."

Then Mrs. Spaulding knocked on the door again, reminding Mr. Perriloux that his other morning appointment was waiting outside. "Well, I hope we can continue this conversation another time, Noah. Keep in touch, okay. And, remember, no more surprises!"

"Okay, no problem," I said. "But do you mind answering one quick question for me?"

"Of course," he said. "Shoot."

"When did you know that you wanted to be a teacher?"

"From an early age, I think. I liked the fact that teaching requires one to place the needs of others before his. That kind of radical selflessness, what the Greeks called *agape*, was inspiring to me. For an old hippie like me, teaching felt like the right thing to do. It still does, actually, but somehow they roped me upstairs."

I actually felt inspired to teach later that day, but when I returned to my classroom a few minutes later, my kids just wouldn't shut the fuck up. All they wanted to talk about was The Vows. *The Vows this, Bands Back Together that.*

"Everyone needs to sit down and fucking be quiet!" I finally screamed, having lost my patience. Not that I was accustomed to having much success in the classroom, but I would've had a better chance of conveying the beauty of Whitman's "Song of Myself" to a colony of apes than I did to their insane asses, so I acquiesced and showed them the DVD of *Dead Poets Society* just to calm them down.

Miles, of course, was in hysterics when he accosted me by the chapel steps at lunchtime, berating himself for skipping school the day before and thus missing all the *Bands Back Together* drama. He grabbed my arm and congratulated me as if I had just given birth to the baby Jesus. "Oh, my God!" he shouted, "I watch *Bands Back Together* all the time! Are you really going to be on it?"

"Yeah," I told him.

"Get out of here!"

"I had to sign a contract. I'm in."

"This is the chance you've been waiting for, right? How long have you known about this shit?" he exclaimed, still grinning like a bastard.

"Miles, watch your language. You can't talk to me like that."

"Okay, sorry. How long have you known about this *stuff?*"

"For a few weeks. They interviewed Tom first, over Winter Break. I knew they were coming."

"Why didn't you fucking tell me?"

"What did I say about your language?" I repeated, afraid that other teachers might hear a student cursing in front of me.

"Dude, sorry."

"And don't call me *dude* either."

"This could be your ticket out of this hell hole."

I couldn't believe what he said next, but he said it. "You need to live large," he exclaimed, his eyes full of passion. Gary Davis Gary, our lead singer, used to say those exact words to me, in the exact same fashion.

"Miles, what did you just say?"

"I said that playing in The Vows is your ticket out of this fuck hole."

"No, after that."

"I don't understand."

"Never mind."

"Stop being weird."

I didn't say anything.

"When and where is the show?" he asked.

"Here in New Orleans, I think, in a few weeks. Everything is still sort of up in the air, but I'm pretty sure they want to film us here."

"You gotta promise me you'll get me in to see the show."

"I don't think so, kid. You're, like, eight years old."

"I'll tell everyone you're banging Miss Sorensen."

He was referring to Chloe, whom I wasn't banging, yet.

"I'm not—wait. Who in the hell do you think you are? You can't threaten me like that."

"I'm only looking out for your best interest."

"What have you heard about me and Miss Sorensen?"

"It's obvious, dude. Bone her already."

Then the bell for fifth period rang, and he disappeared into a blur of fast-moving students. When I turned around, still smarting from Miles's threat, I caught a student whom I didn't know snapping a photo of me with his iPhone. When I gave the kid two days of detention, he asked if he could have my autograph.

Track Four

Later that night Chloe kept pegging me with questions about The Vows. I was busy dispatching my filet and puffy fries at Galatoire's and wanted to keep the conversation centered on something light, as in her plans for the upcoming Carnival season. We were on our infamous third date, the one in which we were, like, *expected* to screw. All I needed to do was make pleasant conversation with her over dinner, take her to Tipitina's afterward so that she could see her favorite local band, and not drink too much. If I could do those three simple things, I kept telling myself, I could crawl in bed with a very beautiful woman for the first time in what seemed like years. Let's just say that I wanted to keep my eye on the ball.

So I kept trying to change the conversation. I didn't want to talk about the band anymore. The conversation always ended up at the same place—why they kicked me out—and I didn't want to become my natural grumpy self. "Did you know that Galatoire's was Tennessee Williams's favorite restaurant in New Orleans?" I asked her.

"No, I didn't, but—"

"Yeah, and that table over there was his favorite table," I said, pointing to the large banquette corner table by the front window. "Noah, come on," she interrupted. "I want to hear more about your experience in The Vows."

"Really?" I asked, trying my best to be polite. I'm sure she could see the strain across my face.

"Why are you being so evasive?" she asked, offering me a taste of her sautéed Trout Almandine. "Is it because your haircut was so bad back then?"

"You're a funny girl, Sorensen," I said dryly, calling her by her last name. But I was beginning to wonder if my former existence in The Vows was the sole reason why she was even out on a date with me. I've been told I'm handsome; people tell me all the time that I look like Sean Penn—rugged, worn, and flaxen—but compared to Chloe I was punching above my weight. Her imperial beauty left her in a class all her own.

"Weren't you guys on *Letterman,* for Christ sake? It couldn't be *that* depressing!"

"They kicked me out of the band. Did you know that?"

"I gathered that, yeah. So?"

I picked up our bottle of wine from the table and began to pour myself another glass, but our waiter, spying me, scurried over so that he could pour the wine himself. When Chloe put her hand over her glass to indicate that she didn't want any more, the waiter poured the remainder of the bottle into mine. "Mike and Gary turned on me like two conspiratorial chess pieces," I told her. "They hated me by the end."

"Who's Mike again?"

"Our bassist."

"Right. I know who Gary Davis Gary is," she said.

I rolled my eyes. "Of course you do," I told her. "Every woman does."

When she asked me if I was excited about the *Bands Back Together* gig, I told her I was optimistic but guarded. I had a lot of questions. *Would we make another serious push at being a band, or were the guys only looking to make a quick buck and then split? Would they even want me back in the band, if we were to reunite permanently? And would I be able to forgive them for kicking me out, if they did?* Until I had answers to these questions, I told Chloe, I wasn't going to let myself get too excited.

I remember her reply, word for word. *No one knows what will happen, Noah, ever.*

She finally changed the subject, thank God, when she asked me what I thought of Miles's music. When I told her that his band's demo was still wrapped in cellophane, unopened in the glove compartment of my car, she didn't laugh. I shrugged my shoulders and let the waiter know that we were ready for our check.

I could tell she had one more question for me.

"Have you ever been in love before?" she finally asked, her face gorgeously lit by the single votive burning on our table.

"Damn, you don't hold back with your questions," I answered, trying to be funny but failing. I could tell from her body language that she was beginning to find all my evasiveness troubling, most likely because her profession involved getting strangers to open up to her about their feelings. But

I didn't like being put on the couch. My father once tried to get me to see every therapist within fifty miles of our house, but it didn't turn out so well. They all told me in various ways that I hadn't gotten over the death of my mother.

"Yes, I've been in love with music, passionately, for as long as I can remember," I told her.

"I meant a *person*. Have you ever been in love with a *person?*"

"Once, yeah."

"She was a musician, I bet," she responded quickly, before reapplying her lipstick. Somehow I could tell that she already knew the answer to her question, so I drained the rest of my wine before saying, "Yes. Agnes Waterstown, the lead singer of The Autumn Set. But something tells me you already know that."

"Yeah, I read about it," she answered, reaching across the table to grab my hand. "It sounds very romantic, to tell you the truth. Traveling to cities together, playing concerts, meeting all kinds of new people. I don't know if I can compete with that."

I didn't take the bait. I knew she wanted me to say something like *you're the hottest woman ever. I'm falling for you already, Chloe.*

"What about you? Have you ever been in love?" I shot back.

"Of course I have. Look at me." I liked her confidence.

"Let me guess. It was with a musician, I bet?"

"Maybe," she said coquettishly, "but not with anyone as famous or as good looking as you." Then she came over to my side of the table and kissed my forehead before heading to the ladies room. She did that thing again—turning around to make sure I was still watching her.

When we finally made it back to her Uptown apartment after midnight, I managed to gain successful entry into her extremely plush bed, with the lights turned off, but each time Chloe and I would kiss, she would stop, sort of hold me, and then ask another question. Unfazed and resolute, I unsnapped her bra.

"I'm up here, buddy," she replied, referring to my eyes still transfixed on her full, perfect, moonlit breasts. I could not have been more erect.

"What did you ask me?"

"You mean before you took off my bra?" she asked.

"Yup."

"I asked if you'd rather play with The Vows or be a teacher at Randolph?"

I thought deeply about my answer, not wanting to fuck it up. Did Chloe want me to be the boyfriend who sacrificed everything so that he could follow his dream (playing guitar with The Vows), or did she want me to be the boyfriend who sacrificed his dreams so that he could make a living (teaching chronic masturbators iambic pentameter and adverb clauses)? Randomly, I remembered Agnes, my ex, saying that musicians aren't like other people because we have passions that we must follow. *Our lives are purposefully and wonderfully wrecked*, I remember her saying one night outside Boston, her tiny fist striking the counter of the late-night diner in which we all sat, waiting for our food. *Musicians can't hold jobs at restaurants or be the fucking manager of The* Gap, she waxed dramatically, *because we all suffer from the same yet lovely curse.* It was those last five words that lingered in my head as I held Chloe's long tall body that night—*the same yet lovely curse.*

"Right now I'm just happy being in your arms, Chloe," I finally told her. "It's hard to think of anything else because I've had a crush on you since the first day I saw you."

Twenty seconds later I had her panties off and my mouth on her breasts and she was running her hands through my hair, saying *Do it, Noah, fuck me* and when I came inside her and was empty, all I could think about again was Agnes. Agnes my ex. *The-same-yet-lovely-curse* Agnes, whom I hadn't seen in years.

"I'm so sleepy, rock star," Chloe said to me, before turning onto her side, her back pressed against me, so that we could spoon for the remainder of the night. *Why is it that the closer I get to someone the more I feel alone?* I remember thinking as I fell asleep.

Track Five

The Vows started like any other band. Tom, Mike, and I each responded to a flyer that Gary had posted on every telephone pole around UT's campus:

Daytime Killer seeks musical geniuses
to dominate the sonic landscape with.
Influences = Velvet Underground, Bowie, Dylan,
The Pixies, Shakespeare and Freud.
Call 534-8976

After surviving a late-night dinner/interview at Kirby Lane, in which we all had to justify our top-five favorite songs and albums, Gary decided that we should next meet at my house for an audition. Tom was a lock to be in the band because he was one of the few accomplished drummers left in Austin who wasn't already in a band. Mike was cocksure and capable on the bass, a virtual sure thing, and the fact that he looked exactly like Flea from The Red Hot Chili Peppers—short, muscular, and crazy-eyed—gave him some sort of instant credibility. Mine came from my equipment—I had a fortress of vintage guitars, pedals, effects sequencers, amplifiers, and a working P.A. Tom later joked *that I could've played like a corpse and still made the band out of pure electronic necessity,* but I more than held my own. Gary put in an outstanding yet typical performance for himself—he showed up an hour late, stoned and shirtless, with three ready-made groupies in tow.

I later came to realize that most musicians spend twenty years looking for the right people to play with, but we were lucky. We were a band from the start. As Tom said, *we slayed ass.* Everyone was happy with the songs I had written (I had a million of them), and we all wanted the same thing—to become the best band in Austin. While most people compared us to Radiohead around that time, we knew our influences went deeper than that, back to the post-punk British New Wave bands like Echo & the Bunnymen, Joy Division, U2, and The Cure.

We played our first show, a New Year's Eve millennium party, under the name Orpheus Descending. A few minutes before midnight, we tore through nine songs—seven originals and two covers—with the energy of a band desperate to prove its mettle. When Gary wasn't banging on his keyboards like a deranged Amadeus, he spun around the stage like a whirling dervish, a young Mick Jagger, making even the most reserved, shoe-gazing hipsters dance. Then, midway through our last song, Mike set fire to a cheap bass guitar he bought that afternoon at a pawnshop on Lamar, sending the crowd into hysterics. After we got called back for an unexpected *second* encore, Gary had to go back on stage to explain that we literally didn't have any more songs to play.

For our second gig, we opened for some clichéd, washed-up alt-country outfit at The Hole in the Wall and blew them off the stage. After our fourth or fifth show, A&R execs were circling us like desperate, hungry cheetahs, and we changed our name to The Vows because we wanted a name that expressed our sense of fight and commitment.

Even though I was a grad student at the time, studying comparative literature at The University of Texas, it was a sea change for me, being in a band. I strode around Austin feeling like a young god, a colossus in corduroy. We practiced every night of the week, getting tight, experimenting and perfecting our sound. Afterwards, Tom, Gary, Mike and I would drive up to Mount Bonnell or hit the bars downtown, sharing stories, smoking cigarettes, and coining phrases. We were becoming an impenetrable gang—a squadron, a platoon, a battleship. It was my imagined life.

It's hard to explain, but even at a very young age I felt that I *experienced* music more deeply than others. I was like a big walking clit, and rock-n-roll was the hand that stroked me. I devoured albums, collected hard-to-find singles, and read all the biographies of my favorite bands and musicians. *The same yet lovely curse* sprouted from my obsession, yes, but my whole being—my entire fucking lonely soul—could be resurrected by the simple act of putting on a record. Music was, for me, my avenue to grace. So being in The Vows meant that my chrysalis had finally been broken. I had become myself—Noah John

Seymour, guitarist and *musician*, twenty-eight years old, from Galveston, Texas.

By the late spring of 2000, when the Texas Hill Country was an idyllic field of bluebonnets, the bidding war for us among record companies escalated to unprecedented levels, as each label was eager to sign Austin's "Next Big Thing." We hired a skilled and experienced music manager, Bill Condon (think General Patton with a cigarette and Budweiser in his hand), who got us a good deal with Slope Records—guaranteed money and full artistic control. After I walked across the stage in late May, my master's degree in Comparative Literature in hand, we flew to L.A. to record our highly anticipated major-label debut album.

But in Hollywood we encountered our first loss, our Manassas. Basically, Gary pulled a total Jim Morrison on us once we got there, being more interested in becoming the new bad boy of the L.A. party scene than getting his shit right in the studio. While the rest of us were sweating it 24/7, feeling the tectonic pressure of making a successful commercial album, Gary had checked out, literally and figuratively, which pissed me off to no end because I really wanted to buckle down and make a great record.

If you don't know Gary Davis Gary by name, then you probably know his face—embarrassingly handsome, a bronzed adolescent god, a young Brando. Yet he was marked, I believed, by some dark brushstroke at birth. Gary Davis (he added the last Gary to his name in an attempt to make his name seem more "rock n' roll") was born into the world on May 10, 1972, in Dallas, two minutes before his identical twin, Drew, was born without a heartbeat, a stillborn. He often complained that his life was stalked by death (this was one of the things that we had in common)—at the age of six he watched his father, an ex-CIA man, get fatally struck by lightning in his backyard, and at fourteen he found his favorite aunt drowned in a bathtub, an apparent suicide. A few years later, after graduating from one of the most prestigious prep schools in Dallas, he knocked a five-year-old boy into a grave with his car bumper. Because the boy had run unexpectedly into the street from between two cars, Gary was able to avoid a vehicular manslaughter charge. But suffice it to say that not a day went by when I didn't see Gary wrestle with his inner-demons, which were large and, to some extent, encouraged by the band because they contributed to his demonic rock-star personality.

One night, on a rare break from the studio, he and I were alone on a rooftop of some Beverly Hills hotel, smoking cigarettes, drinking tequila, and pondering how few stars were visible in the nighttime sky of Los Angeles. Because Gary was standing directly in front of a florescent light bulb as he spoke, a bright luminescence radiated around his face, as if he had finally become the mystic visionary he fancied himself to be. He was unusually animated that night, and the myriad insects swarming around the light bulb appeared to be flying in and out of his head. "The problem with you, Noah," he said confidently, "is that you don't know how to relax and get your head out of the worry box. One day you're gonna wake up bored and shitless."

"Shitless? " I asked laughing, shrugging him off. By that point in the evening, I was pretty wasted. The empty shot glasses on our table looked like discarded shotgun shells.

"Your hesitancy, man, your routines. It's like you're waiting for someone's permission to feel alive. You've got to live large," he exclaimed, exhaling a long thin cloud of smoke into the night air. That was his expression for everything that summer—*to live large.* He said it around twelve times a day.

"Well, if banging skanks and getting high is what I should be doing with my life, then I don't—"

"You know, Noah, just up, up, and up," he interrupted, twirling around and screaming into the dim wheel of stars above him and attracting the attention of everyone at the bar. "Look at this shit. We're signed to Slope. We're making a kick-ass album and standing on the roof of some fucked-up hotel, overlooking a beautiful city. You shouldn't be dead to this. Relax."

I told him that I was stressed because I didn't want our album to fail. *We only have one shot,* I remember saying, *one shot.* But he just kept repeating, "*Live large,* man. Our album is going to kill."

I reminded him that he hadn't been to the studio in a week.

"You're stressing everyone out," he answered. "This is supposed to be fun, you know, being here. This is what you wanted. Remember? I never worry about the band because I know you're worrying enough."

Indie Darling

So that's him in my memory, Gary Davis Gary, twelve floors up and accountable to nothing except his ever-present desire to *live large*. I envied his spontaneity and energy, for sure, but at the same time I recognized an element of self-destruction in nearly everything he did. Even though we shared the same taste in music, we were polar opposites in personality. Gary was fearless and took the raucous energy of our live shows and let it carry over into his personal life, whereas I kept myself in check and simply went back home to write more songs. *Living large*, to me, meant figuring out how to make The Vows a better band, not banging groupie pussy every night or hanging out at some trendy bar until four in the morning, pissing away my talent and creative energy.

But all my fears about failing in the studio came true one night when Edward, our fat-assed A&R guy, said that *he couldn't hear a single*. When I heard those words coming directly from his cocaine face, his thin lips and fat ass, I laughed out loud because it was so fucking cliché. "Open your ears, man," I answered him. "We have *nine* singles on this album."

"Whoa, Hollywood," he replied, "Don't get so nasty."

Hollywood was his nickname for me, that bastard.

"Don't tell me that you can't hear a single when nearly every song is a single," I bristled.

"But I don't hear a *guaranteed* hit, Hollywood. Any one of these songs could get ignored by commercial radio. Times are changing. Radio is changing."

Then I lost it. "Well, you can go fuck yourself then," I uttered childishly before heaving my guitar across the room, barely missing Tom's dreadlocked head.

"Way to go, man," Edward said. "Very fucking professional. I'm just trying to do my job here. We gotta be professionals."

Never one to back down from a fight with his *Don't-tread-on-me* attitude, Mike came to my rescue, for perhaps the only time in my life. "Why don't you get your Backstreet Boys ass out of here before I push your face into the goddamn toilet," he said, walking toward him.

When Edward stormed out of the studio and didn't come back the following day, we waited for the proverbial hammer to come down on us hard, but Condon, our manager, did some solid damage control over at Slope and even got us a new A&R guy (another dick but more benign). Eventually, however, all of this "no single" nonsense from the record company became a complete non-issue when late one night in the studio, I came up with the guitar riff and lyrics for "She Is So Deep."

> When she comes, it's such a big surprise
> She owns you, controls you with her eyes
> Ah, but it's getting later than you think
> She is so deep, she is so deep
>
> She moves you down a hallway of mirror
> Leaves you with the notion to get near her
> Ah, but it's getting later than you think
> She is so deep, she is so deep

Yes, I know I'm not Shakespeare. I wasn't even trying to write a song that night—I was just fooling around with my new

'69 semi hollow-bodied Telecaster, trying to figure out one of Stevie Wonder's bass lines. Apparently, Tom and Mike nearly killed themselves running into the room to play along with me. In less than a minute, Tom added his famous rat-tat-tat drumbeat, and Mike fingered an inventive bass line. When we had the tempo right, I stepped up to Gary's microphone and sang the melody buried inside my head. Ten minutes later, when Gary came back from taking the longest shit of anyone's life, I scribbled down the lyrics for him, and we recorded the entire single right there, live, in three takes—"She Is So Deep," our Billboard and college-radio hit, two minutes and fifty-four seconds of pure rock-n-roll, a serendipitous honeyed gift, a total accident.

"There's your fucking single, Mr. Record Company Man," Mike said, grabbing his crotch and trying to hump everything around the room like a deranged idiot.

"Looks like I can pay back my student loans after all," Tom added, knowing that we had a sure-fire hit under our sleeve. Gary, of course, was more reserved, saying, "I guess that one will do," before leaving the studio to go to another party. But writing and recording "She Is So Deep" gave us the second wind—and confidence—we badly needed. Unfinished threads of songs were finally sewn together, crucial decisions were made, and our album was saved. After another three weeks of stressful mixing, we finally had an album that we all cooed over and tickled like a newborn—*The Weary Boys*. I couldn't wait for the world to hear it.

But on the very day it was released, things began to fall apart.

I was jittery that morning, I remember, because I was in the midst of another failed attempt at quitting smoking, and Gary and Mike's house on Duval Street, where we had met to discuss how we were going to spend the next year supporting the album, smelled like a combination of stale cigarettes, condoms, and wet dog. Condon began the meeting by saying that Slope, our record company, wanted us to go on the road and open for Crookshank, who were also on Slope, yet a few albums past their prime. Gary, however, bristled at the idea, saying, "We need to be out on our own, playing our own shows, not opening for some lame-ass grunge band."

"Yeah, they're a fucking lame-ass grunge band," Mike said, who had become Gary's bitch by then, before giving Gary a high-five and staring directly at me. But Condon and I held our ground, pleading that we couldn't afford to flop financially on the road because we had, within a year, already amassed a considerable debt to Slope in recording the album and making the video for "She Is So Deep."

"I don't give a shit," Gary answered, motioning to Mike and Tom for support. "This is *our* time. I'd rather sing for the twenty people who come to see us than play in front of someone else's crowd."

"Yeah," Mike replied, nodding with his psychotic eyes. "Let's do our own tour. Screw Crookshit, Crookedshaft, whatever. They're douchebags, every one of them."

"You haven't even met them," I responded dryly. "We don't have to spend time with them. We just have to *open* for them." I turned to Tom, to ask him what he thought, hoping for some allegiance.

"I think they're right, Noah," he responded, pulling his dreadlocks down in front of his eyes. "I think we should do our own tour, play clubs in college towns. We're good at that."

"I'm not in this band to make money. Are you?"

This was Gary, of course, speaking to me.

We opened for Crookshank a few weeks later in Athens, Georgia, but Gary and Mike just didn't want to be there, and it showed. Our shows lacked energy, vitality. Then, much to everyone's chagrin, Gary started threatening to quit the band all together, embarrassed at having become a genuine American celebrity overnight, a consequence, we all thought, of Slope using his good looks to promote the album. Gary's face was *everywhere*—on TV, in magazines, in the subway, at Target. I remember him telling one journalist at the time that he couldn't go anywhere "without being bombarded by the clingy, unoriginal adolescents of America."

But we were riding a wave of serious popularity. *The Weary Boys* was appearing on nearly every critic's list for Best Album of the Year, and "She Is So Deep" reached number nine on the Billboard Top 40 chart. Our shows, lethargic as they were, were *packed*. Six hundred people would pay to see us play then leave before Crookshank even took the stage. Our fans' early departure was a little embarrassing for us, yes, but we didn't feel too badly about it, mostly because we never got along with the guys in Crookshank in the first place. But one night outside of Asheville, someone from Crookshank spray-painted the words *The Bowels* on our bus in big green letters. Gary, already being pissed off about having to open for an inferior band, stormed back into the club and pushed over a stack of their amps in the middle of their set, effectively ending their show for the night.

I knew that the lead singer of Crookshank, David Liebling, was a huge asshole—a legendary asshole, in fact. When I was a senior in high school, my best friend and I snuck out of our houses to see a Crookshank concert at the height of their popularity. After the show, I headed home, but my friend waited in the club's parking lot, in the freezing rain, to get someone from the band to sign his vintage Crookshank T-shirt. Apparently, David Liebling came out of the club first and walked right past my friend, telling him to *fuck off*.

So when I saw a very angry David Liebling storm onto our bus the night Gary pushed over their amps, I felt pretty confident that the proverbial shit was going to hit the fan. "Why the fuck did you push over our amps, Gary?" David barked at him angrily, veins popping at the sides of his neck as though he were belting the chorus of one of his songs.

"Why the fuck did you paint that shit on our bus, David?" Gary replied, mocking his tone and demeanor. A few of our fans had gathered by the side of our bus to see what was going to happen next. Even Condon had come out of the bathroom, mid-shit, I believe, to observe, as well. Mike stood behind Gary, repeatedly touching his two fists together, like a boxer about to spar.

"I'll tell you why I painted that shit on your bus," David answered angrily. "And I say this to all of you. You're the fucking opening band, not the fucking Rod Stewart!" After Tom started laughing, David continued, "I've never known any opening band that plays *two* fucking encores. Pay your dues, fuckheads. But do it quietly."

"We only play two encores so that the crowd will leave happy," Mike said, standing behind Gary. "You know, give them a bang for their buck because your band sucks, bud."

"Watch it, asshole," David interrupted, his hands becoming two tight fists. By then, the rest of Crookshank had stepped onto our bus and were saying things to Gary like, "What the fuck did you just say, faggot?"

I stood up, anxious, my heart pounding. I hadn't been in a fistfight since the third grade, so I wasn't sure how I'd fare in one.

"Guys, chill out," our roadie Stuart said earnestly, smiling and handing a bottle of beer to David in a gesture of peace. When David slapped Stuart's offering to the floor, Gary punched him.

The fight was over in about fifteen violent seconds.

"Jesus," Mike said afterward, pointing at my face. When I looked down, my shirt was covered in blood. Crookshank's drummer had elbowed me in the nose, like a bitch.

"I'm gonna kill those motherfuckers," Gary yelled out the window.

"Let it go," Condon said. "It's over."

But Gary turned to me, his breathing still hard, and asked, "Are you happy, Noah, making us play with those assholes?"

"Uh, no, not at the moment," I responded dryly, my hands cupped under my nose to catch all the blood that was pouring from it. Gary stormed off, and Mike followed him out, of course, leaving Tom, Condon, and me to deal with all the blood and the broken glass and the cab ride to the hospital.

After a few more shitty shows, Condon convinced Slope to book us our own cross-country tour the following spring. Quite frankly, we were ready for a break. By the time our vandalized bus rolled back into Austin—*The Bowels* still painted in huge green letters on the side—Gary was threatening to never sing "She Is So Deep" again.

Track Six

My father—the only person in the world who could keep me sane—passed a few weeks later, from leukemia, around Christmastime of that year. None of the guys—Tom, Gary, or Mike—came to his funeral. I traveled a bit afterward, to get my head together and to begin writing songs for our next album. When we finally reconvened in San Francisco, in the spring, a few days before embarking on our very first cross-country tour, my happiness of finally being reunited with the band came to a halt when I learned that Gary, Tom, and Mike had been jamming without me, back in Austin, during the band's break.

"Look, don't take it the wrong way," Tom explained as the elevator door closed on us before we ascended the three floors to the practice loft Condon had rented for us in the city's Marina District. "Gary wrote some songs over the holidays, and we've been working on them a little bit."

"Who fucking played guitar?" I asked.

But Tom didn't tell me the whole truth, saying, "Gary, ha-ha. But you can imagine how that went, huh?"

"Why didn't you guys call me and tell me you were working on new stuff? I would've made it."

When the elevator door opened, I saw Gary untangling a million wires at his keyboard, his hair shaggier and longer than before. He looked like a handsome Bob Dylan circa 1970. I think he might have been wearing a blue polyester shirt, too. "I'm sorry about your father, Noah. I meant to call," he said before walking over to shake my hand. "Did Tom tell you that we've been rehearsing some new songs?"

I spied Mike across the loft staring at me with the crazed eyes of a psychotic assassin. He, too, had some new bullshit 70s look, having dyed his long hair and goatee chalk white. He looked like a fucking idiot wizard in his bellbottomed pants. "Gary wrote a fuckin' rock opera, man," he exclaimed proudly, also coming over to shake my hand and offer condolences about my father.

"A rock what?" I asked matter-of-factly, trying to conceal my disappointment. I was looking for my guitars. I wondered if Condon had even packed them.

"A rock opera, man. It's like *Tommy* or something," Mike answered, strapping on his bass, ready to jam.

They asked me to sit down and listen to Gary's new songs. The first one they played, "Why Were You There," was built around Mike's monotonous, fuzzed-out bass line, like the heartbeat of a wounded elephant that refused to die, echoed only by the sound of Gary striking—over and over—two or three notes on his distorted keyboard—a very minimalist composition. The second song—the best of the bunch—was an unconscionable, note-for-note rip-off of a Pavement song, a lawsuit waiting to happen. The third and fourth songs featured Gary on the electric violin even though Gary didn't know how to play the electric violin. When they began their fifth song, a decent blues-based number that morphed into a heavy-metal free-for-all at the end, I had to pretend I was tying my shoes to keep from laughing. When they finally finished and set their instruments down, all exalted as if they had just won an Olympic relay race or something, Mike turned to me and asked, "Well, what do you think? Fucking talk to us, man. We've been working hard."

"Well, I don't know," I fumbled, re-tying my shoes again. "I'm not sure those songs sound anything like us."

"You say that as though it's a bad thing," Gary responded briskly.

We had had this argument before. Before the band's break, Gary told anyone who would listen that he really wanted "to fuck things up" on our next album and take the band in a whole new musical direction. I didn't pay much attention to him at the time because I was the one who wrote our songs, not him. If I wanted our next album to sound like *The Weary Boys*, then it would sound like *The Weary Boys*.

But Gary kept demanding that we go in a different musical direction, saying that real music was being made by unsigned, unheralded indie bands—bands who *purposefully* resisted commercial success. While I had a certain amount of respect for those guys, in my opinion we were competing with The Beatles and U2 for the best band of all time—not for *the best obscure band no one had ever heard of*. Can you imagine legends like Otis Redding or Bob Marley wanting *fewer* fans? Did

Mick Jagger's desire for success make him an asshole? No, it didn't. But I had a hard time convincing Gary of that fact because his sudden fame, and the negative consequences of it, had been fucking with his shaggy, dirty head. "Your songs might be too violent of a departure from what's made us successful," I argued again, looking for a way to express myself without pissing him off even further. By that point in the conversation, Mike wasn't even listening to me anymore. He was cutting his toenails or something. "Tom, what do you think?" I asked diplomatically.

But Gary interrupted, "I knew you'd say this. I put a bet on it."

"Look," Mike argued, coming back to the conversation. "It doesn't matter if the songs sound like us or not. If they're good, then there's no problem. I see no problem, Noah. There's no fucking problem."

Then I was forced to play my awful hand. "Well, I'm not sure that those songs *are* good, to tell you the truth."

I watched Gary put his violin back into its case, grab his cigarettes from his keyboard, and walk out. Mike, of course, followed him into the elevator without saying a word. When the door closed in front of them, Tom turned to me, and for the first time in the history of the band, I noticed that he was looking at me with the same set of disapproving eyes as Gary's and Mike's. He pointed over to where Gary and Mike had been standing.

"Don't tell me you *like* those songs, Tom. There's no way you could."

"We need new stuff to play. Do you have any songs?"

I only had one, I told him, but it had potential.

When Gary and Mike came back to the loft thirty minutes later, stoned, I'm pretty sure, I convinced Gary to take a walk with me. We found an empty bench alongside the wharf in full view of my favorite monument in the world—the Golden Gate Bridge. With Gary's dark Ray-Ban sunglasses and his longer, shaggier hair, I congratulated him on looking more and more like Bob Dylan. "From which era?" he responded, smirking, his voice letting me know that he didn't mind the comparison.

"I'd say early seventies, for sure. *Blood on the Tracks.*"

He smirked again, lighting up another cigarette—a self-rolled number, of course. By that point, Gary had forsworn anything corporate. For him, it was no longer about *living large* anymore; it was about eating local, buying local, staying local, writing shitty rock operas local, pissing me off local, looking like Bob Dylan local. "I'm sorry about what I said about your songs. I just don't think that they sound like us at all," I told him.

"That's what I like about them. They're *different.* Great artists push boundaries, find new ways of expression."

"Look, we're not Salvador Dali. We're an alternative rock band. What did Bono say about music? *Three chords and the truth?*"

"Your mind is the only thing that's limiting us. We need invention."

Invention my ass, I thought to myself. Some things don't need to be invented, like the Ebola virus or the Holocaust.

"You don't like my songs because they're not the usual, safe, condomized songs you hear on the radio," he continued.

"Condomized?" I asked playfully, trying to make him laugh.

"Yeah, pre-packaged and safe for the kids," he added. "*Condomized.*"

I wanted to tell him that without my non-inventive songs, he'd be back in Austin pimping espressos and over-priced bagels to all his adoring hipsters at Little City, but I didn't. I kept my dirty little condomized mouth shut.

Track Seven

The band did agree on one thing. Getting The Autumn Set to open for us on our cross-country tour was probably the best decision we had ever made. Simply put, The Autumn Set featured four of the hottest women in the history of rock n' roll—Agnes Waterstown, Gail Simmons, Maya Redenbacher, and Anne Spalding.

As fellow musicians from Texas, we knew them well, having shared a bill with them for our first SXSW gig. Afterwards, we formed a mutually beneficial pact—once a month we would travel to Dallas to open for them in front of their home crowd, at Trees, and then a few weeks later they would drive down to Austin to open for us, at Liberty Lunch. Led by Agnes's soulful voice, The Autumn Set played innovative folk rock laden with horns, piano, and strings. Their single "Don't Drown Me Out With Your Bad Shit" was probably my favorite song that year, its moody hip-hop/R&B beat textured with a softly distorted guitar and a mournful trumpet that echoed Agnes's lead vocal.

To my surprise, Agnes and I hit it off from the beginning. A slender, doe-eyed brunette with a pixie haircut, she gushed over my collection of vintage guitars the first time we met, and the next day we spent an entire afternoon flirting in every music store in Austin, trying to find her a Strat like mine. Our friendship developed even further when she started giving me personalized mix tapes each time we saw each other. Tom, being the immature ass he was, never stopped giving me shit about it, proclaiming that her mix-tape gesture was *indicative of the sure fact that she wanted to suck my dick*, but I knew an impenetrable wall existed between Agnes and me—a boyfriend, some quasi-famous painter dude who went by the one-word name Michal. *Whatever.*

So when I saw Agnes in San Francisco the day before our tour began and she didn't have a new mix tape to give me, I felt a little sad. I had woken early that morning and was swimming laps in the outdoor pool of The Phoenix Hotel, which is where any self-respecting rock star would find himself while in San Francisco, when I spied her at the edge of the water, sexy yet blurry as ever.

"Noah, hey," Agnes said, dipping her toe into the water to test out the pool's temperature. When she lifted her dark sunglasses from her eyes, I could tell that she had been crying—her big brown eyes were puffy and wet.

"What's wrong, Agnes?" I asked, wiping the chlorinated water from my own eyes.

"Oh, not much, ha."

"You're crying."

"Yeah."

When I lifted myself out of the pool to sit beside her, the down rush of the water made my loose-fitting swimming trunks fall to my knees, exposing my junk in the cool morning air. I'm sure I looked like a champion moron trying to get my shorts back on as quickly as possible, flailing around like an idiot. Agnes could barely compose herself. "You always know how to make me laugh," she said, putting her arms around me after my trunks were secure around my waist again.

"I'm always here to show you my balls or something."

"Don't worry. I didn't see anything," she said, smiling, but I knew she had.

"Yeah, but I'm not sure those cleaning ladies didn't." I pointed to the two hotel maids who were laughing at me on the second-floor balcony.

"You should charge them for the peep show. They saw the balls of Noah Seymour for free."

"Fuck off."

"You've got nothing to be ashamed of there, cowboy. Settle down."

Her nasal passages were still clogged from her crying, as though she had a cold.

"Oh, I forgot to tell you something," I said excitedly.

"What's that?"

"Fuck off."

I quickly found out the reason for all her crying—she had been up all night on the phone with Michal, who, for some reason, suggested that they put their relationship on hold while she was on tour with us for the rest of the year.

"Hey, Noah! Who the fuck swims in this weather?" shouted Maya Redenbacher, The Autumn Set's red-haired multi-instrumentalist, who was walking towards us from the other end of the pool. Our idyllic privacy had been breached.

"Hey, Maya, what's up?" I asked her, jackhammering my ear to get more water out.

"I was thinking we hotwire a car today and drive out to Napa together," Maya joked. Our tour didn't start until the following night, at The Fillmore, so it was a possibility.

"I'm in," Agnes said, turning and looking at me.

They were asking me if I wanted to go.

"I need to be at a radio station to do an interview around seven o'clock," I said. "Can we be back by then?"

"If we boogie, baby," Maya said.

As we bore down Interstate 80 to Napa, I felt happy in the backseat, finally, my feet dangling out the window, as I watched the sun race beside us, attempting to keep pace with the car. Being twenty-nine at the time, I had the sudden hope that this warm, easy feeling of contentment and self-assuredness is what my thirties would be like. I felt talkative, so I sat up.

"Anyone up for a game of Twenty Questions?" I asked them, reaching for Agnes's acoustic guitar that she had brought with her. I started playing the chords to "Clouds," the song I had written for the band over the break.

"Play louder, cowboy," Agnes joked. "I can't get anything good on the radio. All they're playing is The Vows."

"Hilarious," I said.

"Okay. You start, Noah," Maya said.

"Okay, I have something in mind," I said.

"Can you buy it in a store?" This was Agnes, flipping through a thick girly magazine.

"Yeah."

"Is there one in the car right now?"

"I don't think so. I haven't seen one yet."

Then Maya asked, "Can one eat it?"

"No."

"Is it Michael Jackson's glove?" Agnes asked playfully. She was an unabashed Michael Jackson fan.

"Um, random. But no," I responded dryly.

"Is it Ronald Reagan?" Maya asked in the same playful vein.

"Oh my God, how did you know? Yeah, it's Ronald Fucking Reagan. You must be a psychic of some sort."

"I like that song you're playing, Noah," Agnes interrupted, her eyes following a line of birds that were disappearing, one by one, into a thick tree alongside the road. "Is that Belle and Sebastian?"

"Fuck me. Do they have a song that sounds like this?" I asked, afraid that my song "Clouds" was a rip-off of some song that I didn't even know.

"No, I'm just guessing. Is that one of your songs?"

"Could the thing fit in the car?" Maya asked, still dedicated to the game of Twenty Questions.

"Yeah."

"Yeah is it one of your songs, or yeah the thing could fit in the car?" Agnes asked.

"Both. Yes to both."

"Was that an official question?" Maya asked.

"Yeah. And that was the sixth, I think."

"Give us a hint. I'm not good at this game," Maya said.

"They are coveted prizes at rock-n-roll shows," I said, staring at the spot on Agnes's neck where the little dark hairs swirled. I loved Agnes's short haircut and slacker sense of style. I'm pretty sure I loved everything about her.

"Tight jeans?" Maya asked, giving off one quick snort like a flare.

"No, and that's question number seven."

"Could it fit in the palm of my hand?" Agnes asked, her voice suddenly growing confident.

"Yeah. Eight."

"Do they come in different colors?"

"Yes. And that's nine."

"Are some made thicker than others?"

"Yes."

"Is it a fucking cock?" Maya blurted in disbelief. "It's a fucking cock, isn't it?"

"No. It's a—"

"Guitar pick!" Agnes yelled before I could say anything else.

"Fuck," I said.

"Am I right?" Agnes asked.

"Yeah."

"I thought it was a cock," Maya said.

"You just wanted it to be a cock, you slut," Agnes said, brimming with delight from her win. "He already said that you couldn't eat it. Duh."

"Oh yeah, I forgot," Maya said, wallowing in her defeat.

Hearing their playful banter, I grew envious of Agnes and Maya's camaraderie. Even though they had been in a band together longer than The Vows had been, they still seemed to be great friends. When I asked them when and how they met, I was surprised to find out that they had attended the same high school together, some ritzy, all-girls prep school in Dallas—Hockadoodle or something. "Did you play music together?" I asked them.

"No, I didn't play back then. But Agnes was in a band."

"Yeah, I played rhythm guitar in a band called Agent 99," Agnes said. "Mostly covers. Chick-rock stuff. The Breeders, Pretenders, Hole. But 'Heart of Glass' was my favorite song to sing."

I asked Maya what Agnes was like back in high school.

"She was beautiful, cool, talented. Same as now, I guess, except she hadn't slept with half the world yet."

"Shut up! You were the one who got gang-banged at prom!"

"That's a lie."

"Fess up. You know it to be true."

"She's lying, Noah, it didn't happen. Agnes is just jealous because I stole her date."

"And who was that?" I asked, laughing.

"Rick Sloan," they answered at the same time, in near perfect harmony.

"Who's Rick Sloan?"

"Some guy we drooled over at the time," Agnes responded.

"But who is now is an accountant," Maya said.

"With a belly."

"And bald."

After a slight pause, Agnes traced her fingers on the windshield. "But he had such long beautiful hair back then. What can you say?"

I sat back, running my fingers through my own long hair.

As we descended into Napa, I was struck by how close the vines were to the road, as though they weren't protected at all from the passing cars. We passed the names of vineyards I recognized from my father's wine collection. *Silver Oak. Merryvale. Opus One.*

After we toured a few wineries and had a pretty good buzz going, we pulled into a little picnic spot on a hill to have lunch. I made my sandwich disappear in about five bites, so I got Agnes's guitar out of the car to serenade them, sarcastically, in the manner of a mariachi. They laughed out of kindness, but they were more focused on their lunches. We were all starving like a pack of wolves in winter.

When I played and sang my new song "Clouds" for them in its entirety, they added a few nice vocal flourishes to the song on their own, instantly making it better. It was as though our perfect day in the wine country had made us a little creative troupe, touched by divine inspiration. But like a dark stain spreading on silk, all my anxiety reemerged when Maya asked me why Gary's friend, Pablo Chavez, had been playing guitar with the band back in Austin, without me. When I told her that I didn't know what she was talking about, she backed off a bit, seeming nervous. "I probably have it wrong,"

I remember her saying, but I knew something was up. Then Agnes chimed in, saying, "I heard Gary wrote a rock opera or something? Mike was telling me about it last night. What's up with that noise?"

"Every fucking day with this band is now a nightmare," I said, trying to keep my cool.

"It's okay, Noah," Agnes said, putting her hand on mine. It felt like molecules were being rearranged in my body.

"A rock opera? I didn't know Gary wrote songs," Maya said, tapping her watch to let us know it was time for us to leave. "Are they any good?"

"Nope," I said, helping Agnes up.

Later, when I arrived at the radio station with only a few minutes to spare before our live interview began, I got the total freeze from the band. No one would even look at me. Evidently, Tom didn't find the note that I had left for him, the one explaining that I had gone to Napa for the day with Maya and Agnes. Right before we donned our headphones and the DJ asked us our first question, Mike accused me of "driving off to Timbuktu on purpose" so that the band couldn't work up a few of Gary's new songs to play the following night. I told him that I wasn't capable of such surreptitious sabotage, but he didn't have the vocabulary to know what I was saying. Then we went live.

In the middle of the interview, after we played a acoustic version of "I Want To Die In San Francisco," I saw Condon in the hallway shaking hands with Pablo Chavez, the guy who, according to Maya, had been practicing with the band back in Austin. He and Condon were laughing and smiling like old friends. I struggled to put it all together. "What the fuck is he doing here?" I asked Gary, my mic on, my words broadcasted live over radio.

The DJ cut to a commercial, pissed off. Then some station manager guy, some asshole, stormed into the room and started yelling at me. I ignored him, waiting for Gary to answer my question. Tom sighed, saying, "We were gonna talk to you about it yesterday, but you went all ape shit on us. Condon thought we should wait until Pablo got here today to tell you that he's joining the band."

When we went live again, the DJ asked me a rote question, I guess to calm me down, but I didn't answer him. Total dead air. It was funny later but awkward at the time. When the interview finally wrapped, Mike and Tom left the studio room immediately. Then it was just me, Gary, and the DJ in the corner, still shaking his head at me. Because I had finally quit smoking cigarettes over the break, all the tension of the evening was becoming unbearable. "Gary," I said plaintively, "am I getting kicked out of the band?"

"We talked about getting a multi-instrumentalist guy to help us out on the road, you remember? Pablo's the guy."

"Am I getting replaced?"

"That wasn't our intention, no."

I'll give Gary credit. Pablo's incorporation to the band was a solid choice, I'll admit. He was a quiet, solid, low-key guy, and we became closer, personally speaking, than I ever thought possible. He had put in a lot of hard work to learn all our songs, and he played his backup role professionally and demurely, insisting on standing near the back of the stage whenever we played. Unfortunately, his presence also meant that the band could start incorporating Gary's new songs into our set lists immediately, starting with our first show the following night at the Fillmore. Obviously I wasn't surprised when those new songs just fucking flat-lined on stage, but Gary, somehow, believed *that we must be doing something really musically interesting if we keep getting such a strange, half-muted reaction from our fans.* I couldn't believe the level of his pretension. However, when the band actually got booed one night in Tempe, after we opened with four of Gary's new songs in a row, Gary started comparing our fans' negative reaction to the flak that Bob Dylan got when he went electric at the '65 Newport Folk Festival. "They fucking hated him for that, you know?" Gary waxed out loud in the back of our tour bus as we headed east through Arizona. "They wanted Dylan to stay where he was. They didn't want him to go electric. But he went fucking electric."

"Yeah, they fuckin' hated him for that," echoed Mike, completing his daily pushups. But Gary was no Bob Dylan, I knew, no matter how hard he tried to look like him.

Speaking of which, I was the one *Tangled Up in Blue* at the time, I remember, because Agnes and I were still squared off in an unconsummated, never-ending, dramatic *flirtship.* Since that lovely afternoon in Napa with her and Maya, we had hooked up a few times, yes, but each time we would start messing around, Agnes would get emotional and stop, claiming that she shouldn't be getting involved with me so soon after putting things on hold with her ex, Michal. Then a few days later, we'd hook up again, kissing furiously like teenagers. I remember one starry night in September of that year, an evening that illustrates the fix I was in. Agnes and I had stayed up late on The Autumn Set's bus, as usual, mired the same taxing conversations we normally had—whether or not I should quit The Vows and/or whether or not she should get back together with Michal. I don't know exactly what happened, but things went farther that night—sexually speaking—than they ever had before. I had just removed my hand from between her legs, her soft downy center, having just put my fingers to furious work.

"Damn, Noah," she said, curling up to me.

"What?" I asked, feigning ignorance.

"That was good."

"Then let's not stop," I said, pressing myself—hard and unrequited—against her leg.

But she turned over, onto her side, and wouldn't talk to me. When I sighed out of frustration, I could feel her start to cry. Then, very earnestly, she appealed for my patience, expressing her regret that she couldn't give herself fully to me. *It's not about you,* she kept saying. And for the rest of the night, we sat there counting stars in the silence, her hand resting on mine, until we woke up some three hundred miles down the road, but no closer to each other than we were before.

The next morning, having returned to The Vows' bus, I found Gary in a fit, barking at Tom in the back, trying to convince him to play more aggressively on one of his newer songs. Gary's confidence in his "rock opera"—now titled *Shebang*—had been bolstered by a recent critic's online review of one of our shows, which said that Gary's songs had taken us in *a new musical direction*, or something like that. I figured Gary must've blown the guy backstage to get him to write that.

As Gary and Tom were arguing, I picked up my acoustic and started playing, very innocently and quietly, my new song "Clouds."

Only Tom acknowledged it. "Is that yours?" he asked me, nodding along and looking at Gary, who had picked up the book that he was reading that summer, *Thus Spoke Zarathustra*.

"I wrote it a few months ago, yeah." I was searching Gary's face for some kind of acknowledgement, but he gave me none.

"It's good. Very catchy," Tom said.

"Thanks."

"What do you think, Gary?" Tom asked him.

"It would be too popular," he said immediately, as though he had been waiting to say it.

"What does that even mean?" I asked him nonchalantly, in a sort of laughing manner, my fingers still sliding over the frets of my guitar.

"It sounds like another "She Is So Deep.'"

I stopped playing. "I'm sorry. I don't understand." I could no longer hide my frustration.

"Your new song sounds like another 'She Is So Deep,'" he repeated slowly, as though I might understand him better once he slowed down his words. He put his book down, went to the floor, and started doing his daily pushups. He and Mike were always exercising. "Look, we've been over this. We need to be less commercial on our next album."

"Like having a successful album is such a pain in the ass, huh?" I asked. Tom started pulling his dreads down over his eyes. I wanted him to back me; I needed his help.

"Selling a lot of albums isn't everything. Lots of bands sell albums. Lots of bad ones too."

"What matters then? *Not* selling albums?"

"Being inventive matters," he said. I wanted to punch him for saying that, for suggesting that my songs weren't inventive. "Okay, note to self," I responded sarcastically. "Stop writing songs that sell a lot of albums. I got it now. Thanks." I couldn't help myself.

Mike had come to the back of the bus by that time. I could see that he was trying to get a feel for what was being said, still in that awkward phase between sleep and full wakefulness. He wasn't baring his teeth at me yet. "Don't be an ass," Gary bristled. "I'm just trying to tell you that I don't want our music to be so predictable anymore. We need to change the conversation."

Tom lit up another cigarette. Mike asked him for one.

"We've become a commodity now, a puppet to dangle in front of kids so corporations can make more money. You don't see that, though, do you?" Gary asked me.

I knew I needed to tell him two things. First, I didn't mind the band changing, as long as I liked what we were becoming. And secondly, his songs were total shit, and that if we ever recorded and released them, we would lose our fans, our credibility, our ability to tour, and our record contract. "So are you in?" he asked me. "We're recording a demo of our new songs next week in Minneapolis, for Slope. Condon just booked us three days in a studio. We wanted to tell you that last night, but you were in that bus with Agnes again."

"Sure, let's do it. I'm in," I said, putting my guitar down, resignedly, hoping that Slope would be the entity that would finally kill *Shebang*. Later that morning, in an empty lobby of a truck stop in Missouri, we watched, with horror, two planes crashing into the World Trade Center.

It was September 11, 2001.

After more planes fell, we made our way to Chicago, seeking some kind of salvation we couldn't name.

Track Eight

I was having a moment.

I was standing in the back of my classroom at Randolph Academy, listening attentively to Amy Holloway read aloud the final paragraphs of *The Great Gatsby*. When she got to the final lines about how we are all like *boats beating against the current, borne back endlessly into the past*, I had one of those clairvoyant epiphanies, where the patterns and themes of my life are suddenly revealed.

"What does that mean, Mr. Seymour?" Julie Everett asked out loud, referring to the final line about the boats.

"Well, I'm interested in what you think it means, Julie. I have an idea, but I'd rather hear what you have to say about it." Then her eyes fell from mine and her shoulders slumped. She just wanted me to tell her the answer, but I wasn't that kind of teacher.

Micah Boyd's hand shot up. Micah was one of my best students—perceptive beyond his years in his Malcolm-X style eyeglasses. "Yes, Micah?" I asked.

"I think the narrator is trying to say that one's past is inescapable. Nick Carraway is referring to the fact that Gatsby tried to fashion for himself a better life, but in the end, he failed. How Gatsby dies while foolishly trying to regain his former glory is a prevalent theme in this book."

"You are so gay. Listen to yourself." This was Stu Kleinschmidt. Anytime a student in the class said something beyond his intellectual grasp, Stu had to belittle him. It was his only defense against his growing stupidity.

"I'm not gay, you asshole."

"Guys, settle down," I demanded, interested in what Micah had just said. "Micah, clarify please. Can you repeat what you just said?"

Micah started again, waxing poetically about how Gatsby's romantic dream of getting Daisy back disintegrated before his eyes "like a snowflake touching water."

"Wow, good insight," I told him.

Then Leslie Hodgin's hand shot up.

"Is what Micah just said going to be on the test?" she asked.

"Yes, it's all on the test," I said dismissively as the bell rang and the students fled their desks. *Was I going to end up like Gatsby, floating in a pool with leaves? Was I just another fool trying to regain his former glory?*

A few minutes later, in true Gatsbyesque fashion, a poetic sadness filled my heart when I spied Chloe in the hallway, parting a sea of love-struck boys standing in her way. Watching her confident stride that afternoon, I had visions of Gatsby at the edge of the water, staring at the green light across the sound, haunted by his memories of Daisy. *How do I say this?*

Chloe and I were done, 86'd, *no mas*. Our budding relationship had been clipped. Two days after I made furious love
to her at her apartment, I had her pinned against the door
to her office, kissing her softly and making her smile, as students knocked unaware on the other side. But the next day
she stiff-armed me like a fullback, proclaiming that it would
be a *grave* mistake to get so heavily involved with a co-worker.
"I have to put my job first, Noah. Too many bad things can
happen," she said.

So when Chloe's twin orderly legs stopped moving two feet
in front of me so that we could talk, it wasn't romance she was
after—she was worried because Miles wasn't at school that day,
even though his mom had dropped him off earlier. My first
thought was that Miles was skipping school because Wilco was
in town, but I kept my mouth shut. I didn't want to rat him out.
"Where do you think he could be?" I asked her, attempting to
re-tie my necktie into a better knot. When she set her papers
down and offered to help me, I brushed her hands away.

"You're doing it wrong."

"You don't think I know how to tie a tie?" I asked, laughing.

"Yours are always a little crooked."

"Lord knows I'm not perfect."

Then she gave up on me, my tie, probably any chance of
a future relationship. "Noah, sorry. Let me start over. I was
hoping you might have some idea where Miles is today."

"We're not married. The kid just follows me around."

"I know that. But Mr. Wilkins says that he's been on-edge
lately," she said, watching me fumble my knot for the second
time. "And he has a D in Mrs. Hebert-Puhn's English class."

"Everyone has a D in Mrs. Hebert-Puhn's class. I think he's just concentrating on his music."

"Have you listened to his band yet? I can't get one of their songs out of my head."

"Yes." But I was lying.

"Well, let me know if you hear anything from him, okay? His parents are about to file a missing person's report on him."

"Wait, you think he's *missing*, as in kidnapped or something?"

"We don't know."

"He's probably just skipping school, don't you think? I know he's done it before."

"We don't know."

Watching her walk away, I was curious to see if she would do her thing again—where she turns around to make sure I'm still watching her, but she didn't. Later that night I received my nightly phone call from Tom, who was busy expressing his "shock and awe" excitement that our reunion gig was less than two weeks away. "It's all so fucking perfect, man," he exclaimed after exhaling his joint. Our conversations normally ended when he finished his joint.

"What's perfect?" I wasn't giving him my full attention because I was trying to finish grading my quizzes on dependent clauses. I couldn't stand to have anything school-related over my head.

"That the band can pick up right where we left off. It'll be like we never even kicked you out."

"Are you fucking crazy?" I asked him, putting check marks next to Jessica Mauldin's perfect answers. "I'll never forget that you guys kicked me out."

"For realz?"

"You sound like one of my students," I said, mocking his choice of words.

"You mean those rich kids you teach talk like me?"

"No, they know correct grammar."

"Eff that," he answered. "Two weeks, baby. I'll see you in two."

I put A's on all the remaining quizzes—without even reading them. I just didn't care. "You know, Tom, I might actually be looking forward to seeing your skinny ass."

"We should definitely make out."

"Why don't you go kiss your wife?" I prodded him.

"Dude, we're married."

"I know. That's my point."

"I don't even remember what sex is actually," he said.

"The world is safer, I guess."

"Shock and awe, man."

"I'm not going to start saying that."

"For realz?"

Click. And I hung up on him.

It was all coming together very quickly. Rudy Silverman wanted to shoot, wrap, and edit our episode as soon as possible, "as in fucking yesterday," he wrote to each of us in an email. Because I was stuck teaching at Randolph—Gary, Tom, and Mike all agreed to come to New Orleans on Mardi Gras weekend, the parade-filled days before Fat Tuesday, to play our gig. Having done their homework on the band's history, the show's producers insisted on booking our show at Tipitina's, the legendary music venue in Uptown New Orleans, which is where I got 86'd from the band nearly a decade earlier.

Ironically, I was headed to Tip's that night to see Wilco, one of my favorite bands. But on my way there, I began wondering if my Gatsbyesque maneuver of trying to regain my former glory was evidence that I hadn't properly moved on with my life. *Here I am, stuck in the place where the band kicked me out. Maybe I should just move on and concentrate on being a better teacher? Maybe our concert will suck anyway? Musically speaking, doesn't every song in reprise at the end of an album pale in comparison to the original?*

I saw Miles in his red hoodie immediately upon entering Tip's. He was standing next to Wilco's soundman at the mixing board, pointing to each knob and asking a million questions. For a moment, I considered texting Chloe to tell her that Miles was alive and well, but I didn't want her coming down here and making a scene. I wanted to watch Wilco, in peace, with my Abita Ambers. But I kept my eye on him throughout the show, to make sure he was fine.

Wilco played two perfect sets that night, highlighting their newer, edgier material. They had really become a great live band. Wonderstruck, I dropped backstage to say hello to my friend John, Wilco's bassist, and I left Tip's feeling happy and excited about my choice—the *Bands Back Together* gig would be my chance at redemption and grace. I fell asleep that night, content and self-assured for the first time in a while, until I awoke to a furious rapture on my front door at three in the morning. *Bam, bam, bam!*

"What are you doing here?"

"Nice robe, old guy," he said, holding a go-cup and a cigarette in his right hand. His jeans were torn at the left knee. I could tell, immediately, that he was blitzed off his ass.

"You shouldn't be here, Miles."

"Helllooooo to you too," he said, wobbling and smiling.

"How did you know where I live?"

"I'm Russian spy," he said, holding his fingers out at me, pointed like a gun. Then he pulled his imaginary trigger.

"Come inside. You're bleeding."

He immediately began rummaging through my shit, going from room to room and stopping at every photograph on the wall. Then he'd mumble something incoherent. I started to worry that he might throw up on my new rug from IKEA, so I brought him over to my sturdy kitchen table. "You weren't in school today, kid," I told him, tapping my fingers on the table so that he would keep his drunken focus on me.

"I don't go to that place anymore."

"Did you get kicked out?" I asked him.

"I quit that place. I fucking quit."

"Oh, so you're a high school dropout now?" I asked him, trying not to laugh because I knew Miles hadn't quit Randolph. Chloe would've texted me if he had, I'm sure.

"Affirmative. Roger that."

"Here, let me have that cup. You need to drink some water."

"Lemme play your guitar."

"It's three in the morning, chief."

"I wanna play the yellow one, the Strat."

When he swiveled around to point at it, I snatched his cup from him and hid it under the table. When he turned back around, facing me, he kept reaching for his cup, as though it might suddenly reappear from thin air. "What did your mom say about you skipping school today?"

"Didn't go home, Mr. Seymour buddy."

He was still looking for his go-cup. I knew it was only a matter of time until he slid from the stool. I was trying to figure out what to do. "You mean you haven't been home at all today since your mom dropped you off at school this morning?"

"Affirmative."

"You haven't called them to let them know you're alive?"

He shook his head *no*.

"So they don't know where you are?" I asked, becoming frustrated with him.

He didn't say anything.

"Around three this afternoon, Miles, your parents were about to file a missing person's report on you." Then, in a sudden combustion of energy, he proceeded to barf all over my fucking table. It took about fifteen long miserable seconds for him to stop.

"I think I'm gonna be sick," he mumbled afterwards, a long piece of drool still hanging from his lips and chin. He was a real sight to see.

"Uh, newsflash, kid. You already were."

"What?"

"You threw up all over my table."

"No, I didn't."

"Okay. You're right. You're fucking right," I said, before leaving to find a towel. I needed to clean up his foul-smelling mess.

"Hey, don't be mad at me. You're always mad at me," I heard him say from my kitchen.

When I returned, maybe from being sick, I don't know, he started to cry. Not a deep uncontrollable sob, but a slow slide of consistent, embarrassing tears. He wasn't even trying to wipe them away. He pulled the hood of his red hoodie over his head. "Miles, I'm not mad at you. It's just that you can't show up here, drunk off your ass, at three in the morning when your parents have been looking for you all day. You're a fucking missing person."

"*You're* a fucking missing person," he responded angrily, in copycat fashion.

"They're probably worried to death about you, don't you think?"

"*You're* a fucking missing person."

I started to wonder if I should call his parents, or the cops. "Look, I think we need to call your parents. Now."

"Why would you do that?" His wet eyes were still staring at me.

"I can't be responsible for you," I said plaintively.

"Why not? You're a teacher."

"But this is not a school. This is my home."

"I'm not going back home. I'm a missing person."

This conversation went on for minutes, until we made a stupid deal. Miles would let me drive him home if I agreed to play a song with his band at one of the awful lunchtime student concerts at Randolph Academy. "They're called Lunch Bag Concerts," he reminded me.

"But I only have to play one song, right?" I asked, lowering myself into my car, eager to get him home. "No, you have to play two songs," he answered, changing the terms of the deal. "And you have to act like you're enjoying it. You can't just stand there like a fucking scarecrow."

"I don't even know your music," I told him.

"I gave you our demo a long time ago."

I kept driving, ignoring him. If he had opened the glove box in front of him, he would've seen his band's demo there, unwrapped. "Well, did you even listen to it?" he asked. When I nodded vaguely, he suggested that I probably didn't even know his band's name. "Missing Persons?" I responded.

He lowered his head, defeated.

"I'm sorry, Miles. I'm an asshole. I don't know the name of your band. And I haven't listened to your demo."

"It's Indie Darling, asshole."

"Just Indie Darling? Or Indie Darling Asshole?"

"You don't even care."

I figured that Miles's parents were rich, but I didn't know that he lived in one of the gargantuan Victorian mansions on St. Charles Avenue. When a massive gate opened in front of his house like a huge sail, Miles motioned to me to drive further into his driveway. But I kept my old Volvo in park, not wanting to deal with his parents. But in no time his mother came flying out of her house, gesturing wildly and making a huge scene. Once she realized that Miles was safe, albeit drunk and disheveled, her full attention fell on me because she needed an explanation as to why I was bringing her son home at four in the morning after he had been missing all day. She had no idea who I was. "Mrs. Lafayette, hello," I stammered, getting out my car to offer her my hand, which she didn't accept. "I'm Noah Seymour. I teach at Randolph Academy."

"Miles, what in the hell is going on?" she barked at him, adjusting her robe so that it closed tighter. "You need to explain this to me. Where have you—"

I interrupted. "Miles showed up at my door about an hour ago. I brought him home when he sobered up and told me where he lives."

"I'm a missing person, mom," Miles said, smiling like an idiot.

"That's enough," she said.

She looked in my direction, coldly.

"Mom, Mr. Seymour was in The Vows."

"Miles!" she exclaimed. "Get inside right now. Go talk to your father. He's been worried sick about you." When they started bickering, I gave Mrs. Lafayette sort of an apologetic look and bolted out of there, nearly backing over their cat on my way out.

Track Nine

The next morning I found a note in my faculty mailbox asking me to stop by Mr. Perriloux's office during my off period. With only three minutes to spare before the beginning of first period, I was a spectacle dashing up to my office on the third floor and then flying back down the stairwell to my classroom on the first floor. When I made it by a whisker, as my father used to say, I saw Chloe waiting for me at my desk, wearing her nervous face again. William Simoneaux and Nick Falba, two of my worst behaved students, were standing behind her and simulating the sex that they figured Chloe and I were having. They were a real class act.

I grabbed my students' *Gatsby* tests from my satchel and told them to sit down and get ready. "This test is going to be long and it's going to be hard."

"That's what she said," Colby Brotherton blurted immediately. When Chloe asked if we could talk outside, in the hallway, half the class started whistling at us as I followed her out. I had *zero* control over those kids. "You look like shit, Noah," she said, standing before me in the empty hallway.

"Is my tie messed up again?"

"Did you get hit by a truck or something?"

"If you want to know, Miles showed up at my door at three in the morning last night. He—"

"Yeah, I wanted to talk to you about that," she interrupted. "I got a call from Gail, his mother, this morning. We talked."

"And?"

"She's pissed. She wants to yank Miles out of here and ship him off to military school."

"And what does that have to do with me?"

"Did you take Miles to some kind of club last night?"

"My God, no. He was already at Tip's when I got there."

"So you just saw him there?" she asked, sounding as if she didn't quite believe me. "You didn't bring him?"

"No, he was already there, hanging over some dude at the mixing board. I didn't even talk to him. Not once."

"Okay. I'm just trying to put all this together. I think his mom thinks that you took him there, or got him in somehow."

"Is that what Miles is telling her, because it's wrong? Is this what my meeting with Mr. Perriloux is about?"

"Yeah."

"Well, look," I said, peeking my head back into the classroom to make sure that my infidels weren't cheating. "My class is taking a test. Can we talk about this later?"

"Yeah, sure."

"Am I getting fired?" I asked her directly.

"I don't know."

When the bell rang and I collected their *Gatsby* tests, I closed the door to my room, dimmed the lights, and logged onto my computer before heading to Mr. Perriloux's office. I noticed that my inbox was clogged with emails from Tom, each one proclaiming, *Hollywood, answer your goddamn phone!!!!!* Reluctantly, I called him back as I headed to Mr. Perriloux's office.

"Mike's dead," Tom said upon answering, without even saying *hello*.

"Not falling for it."

"He died yesterday in Austin."

"Nope."

Click.

When I got to Mr. Perriloux's office, he was occupied, of course. So I chatted with Mrs. Spaulding, his secretary, who kept insisting that Mr. Perriloux would be free in a moment and that I should wait for him. She spoke excitedly about the girls' volleyball team, and I had to pretend that I gave two fucks about their recent successes. Finally, Mr. Perriloux's door opened, and I spied five people sitting stiffly in his office—Miles, Chloe, Miles's mother Gail, Mr. Perriloux, and the assistant principal Mr. Dick Knowles. Suddenly I regretted not shaving or showering that morning. I'm pretty sure I even had some of Miles's vomit on my pants' leg from the night before, I can't remember.

"Wat up, old guy?" Miles said to me as I took the empty seat next to him. He even tried to high-five me.

"Mr. Perriloux," Miles's mother said very carefully, "let me be frank, please. I'm not one of those people who likes to blame others, but ever since Miles befriended Mr. Seymour, his attitude and actions have changed, for the worse."

I tried to defend myself.

"This is not your time to speak, Noah," Mr. Dick Knowles said, cutting me off. It was clear that he was leading the administration's witch-hunt against me. Mr. Perriloux only sat very quietly at his desk, eating his carrots.

"No, she's right," Miles chimed in. "I have changed."

"Miles?" I said, shocked.

"I mean that you have influenced me in a good way," he clarified, smiling. "That's all I'm trying to say." His comment went up his mother's ass sideways. "Do you mean to tell me that skipping school and not calling us and going to adult clubs and getting drunk and playing your guitar all the time when your grades are going to pot is a good thing?" she asked.

"Yeah, I think so," Miles replied.

Jesus Christ, this kid, I thought to myself.

"What's wrong with you, son?"

"You want to know what's wrong with me?"

"Yes," his mother said. "Please."

"I'm *happy*. That's what's wrong with me. I jerk off. I wear weird clothes. I play guitar. I'm different than you."

Mr. Perriloux covered his ears.

"Watch your mouth, son," Dick Knowles ejaculated, referring to Miles's comment about masturbating.

"I don't want to be like you," Miles continued, having broken down a bit emotionally, out of frustration. "With your TV shows and your shopping malls and your affair with that old guy."

"Miles!" his mother exclaimed. "Mr. Flynn and I are just friends."

"Yeah, you right. He's just a friend—a friend I saw you going down on in the laundry room."

"You will stop this! Now!"

"You want me to be like you and dad, but you're already dead." I watched him collapse into his chair. I looked over at Chloe, hoping that she'd come to his rescue, but she merely uncrossed then re-crossed her legs. "Already fucking dead," Miles continued, looking like he was about to cry.

"Are you suicidal, Miles?" Dick Knowles asked him directly, taking out his handkerchief and passing it to Miles's mom.

"I'm not Kurt Fucking Cobain," Miles exclaimed.

"Or Ian Curtis," I added. Everyone—Mr. Perriloux, Dick Knowles, Gail, and Chloe—gave me a stern look *no*. I knew I had made a mistake, saying it.

"Or Fat Elvis," Miles responded quickly, responding to my joke and wiping away his tears.

"Did you do drugs or drink alcohol with Mr. Seymour last night?" Dick asked.

"No," Miles answered. I raised my hand to say something, but Dick motioned me off with his arm. I wanted to slap him.

"Did you?" his mother replied.

"Did I *what*?" Miles asked.

"Do drugs or drink alcohol with Mr. Seymour last night?"

"He doesn't even do that stuff," Miles exclaimed, looking at me.

"Don't lie to us," his mom said. "We know everything."

"No, you don't. You should be trying to find out what a great teacher Mr. Seymour is. He's the only one around here who knows what's going on. He's the only one who's real."

His words were flattering, but I didn't believe them. I wasn't a good teacher. I hadn't made a single kid's life better at Randolph. I knew that.

"You're going to fire him, aren't you?" Miles asked Dick Knowles, who looked at Mr. Perriloux. When Chloe said something cliché about the pitfalls of carrying around too much anger, Miles stood up to leave. "Can I go back to Western Civ, please?" he asked. "I don't want to fail any more tests. I wouldn't want to make my mom the adulterer mad at me."

I, too, was dismissed after another round of questions. When Mr. Perriloux said that he wanted to speak to me again later that day, I figured he just wanted to fire me in private. Once I returned to my darkened classroom, waiting for third period to start, I listened to a voicemail from an unknown number originating in Beverly Hills, California. I had a good idea whom it was from. When I called the number back, Gary Davis Gary answered on the second ring. He was playing the first measure of "I Want to Die in San Francisco," my favorite song from *The Weary Boys*, on his keyboard. At the time, I didn't see the irony of it.

"Hollywood," he said. There was more goodwill in his voice than I expected.

"It's been a long time. What's up?"

"Mike died yesterday," he answered, striking what sounded like a D minor on his keyboard.

"Tom already tried that one on me. I'm not falling for it. I'm—"

But it turned out to be true. On the same day that Miles skipped school and threw up all over my kitchen table, a city bus slammed into Mike as he pedaled through downtown Austin on his way to work. Apparently, the bus pummeled Mike so hard that his head literally flew off his body, such was the brute force of the impact. I still don't know how that's scientifically possible, but it happened. I couldn't make that shit up. *In pace requiescat,* as Poe wrote.

"Fuck," I said. "Really?"

I didn't know what else to say.

"Yeah, it's not a joke."

"I guess not. When is the funeral?" I asked absentmindedly, still trying to wrap my head around what happened.

"In a few days. I'm not sure I can make it. I'm trying to wrap up a few things here before I head down to New Orleans."

"You mean his head fucking flew off his body?"

"That's what I heard. Why?"

"Tom told you that?"

"His mother did. I talked to her this morning."

"Fuck."

"I know."

Students had begun to congregate outside my classroom and were making faces at me through the window in the door. I lowered my head and shuffled some papers. "Does Rudy Silverman know yet?" I asked.

"I don't think so."

My mind started filling with weird trash.

"I talked to Mike's mom. She thinks we should still play our gig because that's what Mike would've wanted," Gary continued. "I was calling to see if you know any bass players in town who could take Mike's place. I know it's short notice."

"Pablo," I answered quickly. Tom was supposed to call him anyway, I told Gary, to invite him to our show.

"Can he play bass though?" he asked.

Smirking, I told him that Mike's bass lines weren't that difficult to play. Then I felt bad because I was insulting the dead. The *decapitated* dead, no less. "Pablo can definitely handle it," I continued matter-of-factly. "We just need to make sure he's not on tour with his band."

Ironically, Pablo was the only one of us still in the game, being a founding and current member of Vinyl, an eclectic folk-pop ensemble with a strange Middle Eastern bent. I'd gotten to see one of their shows a few years prior, a surreal vaudevillian affair, right after Katrina, when they came through New Orleans. Pablo and I got smashed afterwards, in the French Quarter, to drown my professional jealousy. We nearly got mugged, then arrested.

"What's that in the background?" Gary asked me.

"The bell for third period ringing."

"That's right. I heard you're a teacher now."

"Yeah, I'm just living the fucking dream," I said sarcastically, motioning to my students to come in, sit down, and be quiet.

"You're like Sting now, except he was a teacher before he was in a band."

"I'm like a reverse Sting," I answered stupidly.

"Can't wait to hear about it."

"Hey," I said. "I'm sorry about Mike."

"Thanks, brother."

Five minutes later, I'm sure I did the worst job teaching T.S. Eliot's "The Love Song for J. Alfred Prufrock" in the entire history of pedagogy because when Prufrock kept going on and on about *"What would it all mean, What would it all mean?"* all I could think about was whether our *Bands Back Together* gig would be cancelled now that Mike was dead. *Even in death that motherfucker can still fuck things up for me,* I told myself. At lunch, in a total fog, I ran into Mr. Perriloux in the hallway. He seemed to be looking for me. *Just fire me,* I said under my breath.

He grabbed me at the elbow. "Help me understand what went on last night, Noah. I don't know what to think, to tell you the truth."

When I told him, for the third time that day, that I had nothing to do with Miles's problems—his truancy or delinquency or depression or whatever—he sat in silence for about five awkward seconds, stroking his mustache. *Fire me, dude. Get it over with.* "Miles is very fond of you," he finally said. "What do you make of that?"

"I don't know, really," I stammered, not knowing what to say. If there's one thing I learned about Mr. Perriloux, it's that he never settled for bullshit, vague answers about school matters.

"Well, maybe you could think of it now?" he asked.

"I think he's fond of me because I was in a band. That's all. But I don't think he knows me very well."

Mr. Perriloux then referenced a conversation we had earlier in the year regarding the concept of *agape*. He reminded me that great teachers give themselves fully to their students and grow to love them unconditionally as real people and not merely as desk-occupiers. "Do you feel like you've grown in that way this year? It's obvious that your students love you a great deal. I've spoken to a few of them today. But I'm curious about *you*. How do you feel about them? Do you want to be a teacher here?"

"Can I be honest with you?"

"Of course."

"I'll finish the year, but I don't think that you should renew my contract for next year. This will be it for me. Sorry."

It wasn't the answer he wanted, but the school's fire alarms started going off, rather loudly. Mr. Perriloux covered his eighty-year-old ears with his hands and flashed a worried expression across his face. *This is no drill,* he mouthed.

Crossing Annunciation Street to the baseball field, I heard the ominous sirens of a fire truck in the distance. I turned back to see if Randolph Academy was, in fact, on fire. Instead, I only saw the lonesome figure of one student on the third-floor balcony who was lowering a homemade banner made crudely from a bed sheet. My stomach fell when I read its green, crooked, spray-painted letters—

EAT A BOWL OF DICKS PEOPLE, SAVE MR. SEYMOUR

A murmur quickly spread through the crowd, and all turned around to see Miles punching the air above him awkwardly, stupidly. Then he dropped his pants, I swear, and mooned everyone, including the New Orleans Fire Department, which had just come roaring into the school's parking lot. Watching two security guards chase him away, I felt sad for him, yes, but also a little relieved, because I had most likely seen the last of Miles Lafayette.

When the bell rang at three o'clock and I bolted out the side doors onto Annunciation Street, the little fucker ambushed me in the faculty parking lot, where he had been hiding between two cars. "Not today, Miles," I barked, making little eye contact with him. Because it had begun to drizzle, I was walking more quickly than usual. "Did you see what I did today?" he asked me proudly.

"It was retarded. Did they kick you out?"

"Yep. About an hour ago. My mom was going to ship me off to military school in Vermont anyway. Did they fire *you*?"

"Nope. Your stunt was for nothing."

"Oh well. *Au revoir*, motherfuckers!"

"Miles," I tried to say sternly, "I don't think you know what you're doing with your life."

"Well, that makes two of us then."

I stopped and looked at him. He seemed worried and oddly out of breath. "Look, what do you want from me?"

"I thought we were friends," he said.

"I'm not your friend. You're fifteen years old."

"Sixteen."

"And there's a difference?"

"Why can't we be friends?"

"I don't have any friends," I told him. I meant it as a joke, but after I said it, I wondered if it was true. I had almost made it to my car. I accidentally hit the panic button on my remote-key thingy, so my Volvo was going berserk in the faculty parking lot. It became clear that Miles didn't want to be seen. I'm sure he was told to vacate the campus—*forever.*

"Do you know anyone who plays bass," I asked him, quieting my car's alarm. I knew that if Pablo couldn't play with us, we'd be fucked.

"James Montgomery," he answered quickly, referring to weirdest kid on campus. James Montgomery was so bizarre that mosquitoes probably fled from him. One of the rumors floating around the school was that he had once used a Snickers wrapper for a condom. Knowing the kid, the story was probably legit. "No, someone a little older. And less fucked up, too," I responded.

"Why?"

"Mike died yesterday."

"Who the fuck is Mike?" he asked, gesturing stupidly with his arms.

"Mike. Our bassist Mike. From The Vows?" I answered.

"Really? No way. He's dead? I bet you killed him, didn't you?"

"He died yesterday in Austin. He was crushed by a bus. His head flew off."

"You probably drove that bus. You probably waxed the guy."

"No, I was with your drunken ass last night. You're my alibi."

Then Miles went around to the other side of my car, as though I was going to let him in. His hair was stuck to his forehead, on account of the rain. "I'm not giving you a ride anywhere, kid. Back up."

"Mike is a missing person now, huh?" he asked coyly.

His joke worked. I laughed.

"See, I'm funny and can make you laugh. I can bring things to the relationship."

"Miles, are you gay?" I asked him. "Is this what this is about?"

"Dude, I'm dating Ann Berg. We've been together for, like, three weeks."

I had seen him in the hallways with an arty, beret-topped girl who perpetually carried in her arms a French II text-book, but I didn't know her name or if they were just friends. "Then why did you get yourself kicked out of here?" I asked.

But he didn't have an answer for me. Instead, he said, "Mr. Perriloux is one old fucker, huh? Every time I talk to him, I think he's gonna die on my ass."

"He's actually a really cool guy," I said, opening my car's door. "I wish you'd look up to him instead of to me. I don't have anything to teach you. He does."

When I drove away without saying goodbye, I felt bad. Miles seemed so alone, standing there in the puddled parking lot with no one to talk to. Then it looked like the rain was making him disappear, as he became this tiny distorted blur in my rearview mirror. Watching him that afternoon, I made a small vow to start treating him a little better.

I was the only one from The Vows to show up at Mike's funeral a few days later. Despite Chloe's protests, I called in sick and got on the road before daylight, making it to the funeral in Austin with only a few minutes to spare. I guess I wanted to honor Mike's life somehow, or get some kind of closure. I don't pretend to know why I do everything I do.

Interestingly enough, the first person I saw in the waiting room of the funeral parlor was Agnes, my ex, who was standing around looking lost, as usual, yet also exquisitely fashionable. She wore a simple black dress with a sky blue scarf, I remember, as well as some kind of vintage headpiece with a veil descending over her left eye. Her short pixie haircut had grown out fully—her long hair was wavy now and resting near her breasts. She looked past me at first, without recognizing who I was. We hadn't seen each other in nearly ten years. "Agnes, hey. It's Noah." I was doing something weird with my hands.

"Holy shit!" she shrieked, making sure that everyone in that dreadful place turned around and stared at us. "I didn't think I'd see you here. Sorry, I'm kind of out of it," she continued.

"It's good to see you. No worries."

We stepped forward to kiss each other on the cheek. "You look great," I told her.

"Noah, this is my husband Roger," she said, introducing the tall man who had just walked over to us. "Roger, this is Noah, an old friend of mine." Roger looked like a dead-ringer for Superman, and he unrolled his man-of-steel hand so that I could shake it. It weighed about fifty pounds. "You were in The Vows, right, with Mike?" he asked, unsure of himself.

"Afraid so."

I don't know why I said that.

"I used to work in the business a little bit," he offered, smiling. His teeth were set perfectly, like masonry.

"You played in a band?" I asked him. Agnes started laughing.

"I was on the corporate side of things. Label-type stuff," he said, looking at her.

"Yeah, sure," I said.

Agnes was glowing. I couldn't get over how gorgeous she looked with her longer hair. "How long have you two been married?" I asked her. "It's been so long since we last spoke."

"Ten years, I know."

It was nine, but I didn't correct her.

Roger spoke up. "We were married two summers ago in Dallas. Plano, actually."

"That's great," I said. Then Mike's mother, whom I had never met, came over and introduced herself. When she realized that I was *Noah from The Vows*, she grabbed me very tightly and didn't stop crying for a while. In fact, for the rest of the afternoon, she treated me as though Mike and I had been best friends since childhood and that no animosity had ever transpired between us. I couldn't decide if she just didn't know the band's history, or if she just didn't care, realizing that we were just kids, basically, when The Vows disbanded. "Mike loved you so much," she kept saying to me, shaking me at my shoulders. "He was so proud of what you guys accomplished."

I started to wonder if she had me confused for Tom. She kept lighting one cigarette after another, and I had to continually tell her that it was okay to smoke in front of me. "I know he was looking forward to playing with you guys in New Orleans in a few weeks," she continued. "When that TV man came to interview him, I hadn't seen him so happy in years. He was so happy, right, Rebecca?" Rebecca was Mike's younger sister. She looked like a female version of Mike—*scary*.

"Yeah," Rebecca answered, "you would have thought that he won the freaking lottery or something."

"Are you guys going to play the concert?" Mike's mom asked. I could tell by the way she asked the question that she hoped that we would. Pablo had, in fact, agreed to come down and play bass for us, so I told her *yes*. I asked them if they remembered Pablo.

"He was your manager, right?" Rebecca said.

Agnes smiled. "Yes," I said, lying.

After the strange ceremony, in which I was asked to play "She Is So Deep" on the guitar while they lowered Mike's casket into the ground, Mike's mom introduced me to every relative of hers who had probably ever existed. I shook about two hundred hands in twenty minutes, feeling less like a conspirator than I did when I walked through the front door of the funeral home an hour earlier. When it was time to leave, I spied Agnes in the corner, alone, waiting for me to come over. We had been making a lot of clandestine, furtive eye contact throughout the funeral, prompting me to wonder how happy she was with Roger. Maybe I'm wrong, but when two ex-lovers make a lot of secret and sustained eye contact over a short period of time, it's the same thing as slipping out the side door and fucking. I didn't need words to communicate my attraction to her. And neither did she, evidently. "So," Agnes said, biting her lip, once I was standing beside her. She was brushing some lint from my shoulder. I wondered if it were possible for us *not* to flirt with each other.

"It's been a long time, huh?" she asked, looking over at Roger, who was on the other side of the room, talking to a group of old men. I kept wondering when he was going to dash out, find a phone booth, change his clothes, and fly off to save a busload of children.

"Too long, in fact. How are you?" I asked her.

"Good. I'm good."

Her voice made me think otherwise.

"I heard you guys are getting back together for that TV show?" she continued.

"*Bands Back Together*, yeah. Have you seen it?"

"No. We don't have cable. I tell Roger all the time that television is the devil."

"That's good, because I'm probably going to look like a fool anyway. I'm sure I'll be made out to be the villain."

"You'll be fine. Just be you," she said, comforting me, as always. I loved seeing her smile.

"Pablo is going to fill in for Mike. He's gonna come down and play bass for us."

"I'm jealous," she said, looking again at Roger. I wondered if Roger knew that we were once linked. "When is your show?"

"Not this coming Saturday, but the one after that," I told her. "The thirteenth, I think. It's at Tip's, if you can believe that shit." I didn't have to explain to her the irony of playing there. "Are *you* still playing music?" I asked her, adding that I had been listening to The Autumn Set's album, *Mucho Mistrust*, that very morning, on my drive over from New Orleans.

"No, and I miss it. I haven't spoken to Maya in years, except on Facebook. Gail is pregnant now, married. Anne lives in Bangor, Maine." Then she paused before adding, "Roger has two kids from a previous marriage, so—"

Then she looked down.

"We're getting old, Agnes."

"Tell me about it. I'm forty next month. I'm like a cougar here, flirting with you." Then she made some kind of pawing motion in the air. My penis began to awaken. We both looked over at Roger, who was watching us.

"I got you beat. I go to bed at nine o'clock now," I told her. "Can you imagine that? We used to go to bed when the sun came up."

She touched my arm and let her hand linger there, saying, "I drive a minivan. A goddamn blue Dodge minivan."

I stammered for a second. "I'm a high school teacher."

"Okay, you win."

Then Roger came over, talking distractedly because he wanted to leave. They each made it seem like they would come to New Orleans to see our gig, with Roger adding that he even had some business to do in the city. He kept asking me if I knew some particular guy, "Mr. Redmann from the Garden District," as though I would know the motherfucker. The last thing I remember was Agnes giving me a kiss on my face and then trying to wipe her lipstick off my cheek as Roger pulled her away playfully. I watched them drive off in their minivan towards Dallas. Another poetic sadness filled my heart.

That night, feeling nostalgic, I drove around Austin a bit before heading back to New Orleans. I looked for the street pole on Rio Grande where I first saw Gary's flyer advertising his desire to start a band. The pole was still there, of course, covered by flyers of newer bands playing in clubs that didn't even exist when we made our debut as a band a decade earlier. *The more things change the more they stay the same*, I thought to myself.

Track Ten

To finish the backstory of the band, I need to take you to an uncomfortably hot afternoon in Memphis, near the end of our cross-country tour. We were all sitting on the rooftop of another fancy hotel overlooking the Mississippi River and showing off our vast, collective knowledge of the noisy, clangorous history of rock-n-roll. The Autumn Set was there, as well as another local band whose name I no longer remember, because they never made it, and Theresa, who later became Tom's wife. The drinks had been flowing heavily since lunchtime, so we were all a little voluble, sweaty, and fussy.

"Okay, the best album of all time?" Agnes asked everyone, but her question sounded more like a dare. All that afternoon, I remember, she looked irresistible—oddly preppy in her turquoise cotton dress, floral pink headband, and loopy string of fake pearls. Agnes could pull off many different looks—preppy, rock-star, vampy vixen, hippie, etc. I both loved and feared the mercurial element in her.

After she pursed her lips in anticipation of our answers, I reached across the space between our two chairs to hold her hand, even though we were no longer hooking up by that point—because she and Michal had officially gotten back together, when he surprised her one night by showing up to one of our gigs in Chicago. I remember screwing up a number of my solos that night, as he stood there watching our entire set with his arm folded around Agnes, the emo-painter bastard.

"That's easy, man, it's *The Wall*," blurted Tom, taking a brief break from kissing Theresa's face. Theresa had just joined our caravan of fools a few weeks prior, in Minneapolis, when she became Tom's first groupie fuck in the bathroom of the club we were playing. She boarded our bus later that night, much to everyone's surprise, carrying two small weirdo suitcases and an old tin lunchbox full of herbal tea bags. Since that night, she and Tom hadn't taken their hands off each other. In fact, they had been having so much sex that Tom, worried that Theresa might have given him herpes, whipped out his dick one night for us to inspect it, but Condon told him that he had just been fucking too much and to give his foreskin a break. Personally, I was glad that Tom had finally gotten a girlfriend, but his devotion to Theresa left me feeling even more isolated on the tour.

"That album is totally weak cheese," answered Maya, The Autumn Set's multi-instrumentalist, referring to *The Wall.* "Fucking weak-ass cheese right there."

"No way, not at all," answered Mike, who was suffering an unrequited crush on Maya. "Plus, the movie they did for that album is pretty good, especially if you're baked."

"That's why Tom likes it," I answered him, squeezing Agnes's hand. "Tom's always stoned. Aren't you, Tom?" But he was too enveloped in Theresa's face to hear me.

Then Gary interjected, "Tom, dude, get a fucking room if you're going to touch her tits out here. This place is a respectable establishment."

"Yeah, I think they have a bidet in the bathroom," joked Agnes.

"There's a negro just sitting there in the men's bathroom," said Mike, the fucking racist.

"Sorry, guys," Theresa said, coming up for air, her own lipstick smeared across her face.

"*Thriller*, bitches," Agnes said, letting go of my hand to make a touchdown gesture with her arms.

"What?" Maya asked, taking another sip of her drink.

"It's *Thriller*. The best album of all time," Agnes repeated.

"Fuck that," said Gary confidently, lighting up another self-rolled, non-corporate cig.

"It's a great fucking album," Agnes replied to him.

"Do you mean it's a great album to fuck to, or a fucking great album?" Maya asked, laughing.

"Both. It's both."

"I'm sorry, but I don't want to imagine Michael Jackson all zombied out in a graveyard when someone's going down on me, no thank you," answered Maya, ever the comedienne. Then she started doing her best impression of that freaky graveyard dance that MJ did in his "Thriller" video. "That shit would freak me out," she said.

"No one wants to go down on you, bitch," joked Agnes.

"Why you gotta be startin' something?" replied Maya, pun intended.

"Just beat it, girl," Agnes said.

"I did this morning, thank you," Maya answered, ending the pun contest.

After I told everyone that *Revolver* was by far the best album of all time, I was curious to see if Gary would say *Blood on the Tracks* or *Blonde on Blonde*, both Dylan albums, because he listened to them all the time. But to my surprise, he said his favorite album of all time was by some unheralded indie German popkraft band that he had just discovered a few weeks prior. I can't even remember the name of the album he named; it was in German anyway.

"That sounds like a Hitler youth record, Gary," Maya said.

Everyone laughed, except Gary.

"Seriously, though, what are you talking about?" I asked him, alcohol limiting my inhibitions. "You just started listening to that album a week ago."

"How the fuck would you know what I listen to these days," he answered. "You don't even ride in our bus," referring to the fact that I was spending more time on The Autumn Set's bus than our own. After Gary said his bitchy comment, it became so quiet that you could've heard a fish fart in the Mississippi River below us. Tom, in order to quell his anxiety, started singing "Moon River" obnoxiously to himself, but screwing up the words—and the melody. Eventually, Theresa placed her finger over his lips to quiet him down. "I'm sorry but I thought you would say *Blood on the Tracks* or *Blonde on Blonde*," I told him confidently. "But, no," I said, trying to be funny, "you have to name some crazy album that no one's ever heard of."

Gary just sat there, trying to seem indifferent. Mike looked like he wanted to kick me in the tits.

"*Blood on the Tracks* is totally better," said Gail Simmons, The Autumn Set's drummer, trying to continue our conversation. "You've got 'Tangled Up in Blue' and 'Shelter from the Storm.'"

"Idiot Wind," I said a little too bitingly, because even Mike was able to catch the irony.

"Fuck you, Noah," Gary bristled, standing up. "I'm sick of all your negativity."

"Gary, chill," Condon said, lighting a cigarette. Then Gary and Mike stormed off, as they always did, announcing they were going to get something to eat. They didn't even ask anyone to join them. Afterward, we all sat around not saying much. I had already finished my drink, so I was just staring at the lonely lemon wedge at the bottom of my glass, wondering whether or not I had won the argument. "You guys need therapy," said one of the guys from the band that was hanging out with us. I think his name was Kendall, or Khalid. Maybe it was Cameron.

"Yeah, tell me about it," laughed Tom, who was still draped over Theresa. "It's Jerry Springer every day up in this motherfucker."

"You can say that again," Pablo said, taking a draw on his European cigarette as he sat on the periphery, as always.

"But he doesn't even listen to that album," I said, beating my dead, imaginary horse. No one was impressed.

When we walked off the stage that night in Memphis, I didn't get all of it, but I overheard Gary saying to the other guys that *it was either him or me* and *that he'd had enough of my ass*, with Pablo trying to convince him otherwise, arguing that every band has its conflicts and that they need to work through them. I kept telling myself that I only needed to last one more week, as we only had three more shows on that tour—New Orleans, Houston, and then our final, homecoming show in Austin—at Liberty Lunch. *Just one more week*, I kept saying, as though it were some kind of mantra.

After we followed the meandering Mississippi River down to New Orleans, we pulled up to Tipitina's with everyone on our bus in a total tizzy. Condon had just received word from Slope that they hated Gary's rock opera, at least our demo of it. The news was, for me, of course, like a dream come true. The president of Slope told Condon that Gary's songs were total shit and that we needed to stick with "better, more relevant and radio-friendly material." Gary nearly self-combusted when he heard that Slope wanted our next album to sound just like *The Weary Boys*.

"More radio friendly?" Gary ejaculated out loud. "Is that what those fuckers said? Really?"

"Fuck Slope," chimed in Mike. "Let's take our demo to Merge or Sub Pop, where we won't be fucked with."

I knew for a fact that Gary and Mike had been scanning my face, attempting to spy some satisfaction hidden there, but I had been careful not to give them any cause for anger. In fact, I was able to keep a straight face for the whole conversation until Mike barked, "I bet if we had recorded Sgt. Fucking Pepper's that Slope would've said the same thing. They don't know shit."

"Did I just say something funny?" Mike asked me, when he saw me smirking.

"I was thinking of something else. Sorry."

"I bet you were."

Later that afternoon, we had our worst sound check ever. Gary and Mike wouldn't even look at me, as though I were to blame somehow for Slope's rejection of Gary's rock opera. Again, I just kept my mouth shut and kept repeating my mantra, but in all honesty, I was nearly ready to call it quits myself, drained from having been on the road for so long. I missed my dad, Austin, my apartment, Agnes—everything. I missed the feeling I had when The Vows first banded together, before all the bullshit and the rock operas and the drama, when we were just four guys free and confident and happy—making great, original music together. I asked Gary if we could go somewhere and talk, but he said he felt a migraine coming on.

And so it all ended with a whimper rather than a bang.

After eating dinner at Casamento's with Pablo, Maya, and Agnes, I walked back to Tipitina's not knowing that I had already played my final show with The Vows. When Gary, Mike, and Tom met me by the bus to tell me with nervous faces that we needed to talk, all my disappointment and frustration came to a boil. I made a quick, sudden fist and clocked Mike in the jaw before he could even say it.

And then I just started walking.

A few months later, after having put down roots in New Orleans, I was surprised to learn that Slope had granted the band its full, unconditional release—a rather bold and unprecedented move for any label, much less for one the size of Slope. But Slope didn't want to touch Gary's rock opera, so they cut their losses. I read the band imploded soon afterward, most likely from a wave of self-doubt after no other label would agree to release *Shebang*.

I had been right, of course. But The Vows was now dead.

Track Eleven

When Tom, Pablo, and Gary finally arrived in New Orleans two days before our *Bands Back Together* reunion gig, I was stuck at a mind-numbing teacher in-service at Randolph Academy. While Mr. Boring-Ass Education Man kept going on and on about his academic *who-gives-a-fuck*, I had visions of Gary, Tom, and Pablo checking into their hotel rooms, grabbing a few beers, and swapping old stories about the band. Already I was feeling left out. I needed to escape—badly.

As if to prolong my misery, I got a surprise text from Agnes saying that she had just landed at Armstrong and was headed Uptown in a cab to find me. An hour later, around two o'clock, I got a second text from her asking if she could sleep at my house for the night until her husband Roger arrived on the following day, because she was having trouble finding a hotel room. Finally, thirty minutes before I was dismissed from the in-service, I received a final text from her saying that she was already at Randolph Academy, waiting for me in the faculty parking lot and wondering where the fuck I was. An hour later, I felt thrown back into my old life—Agnes was sitting beside me in the front seat of my car, and I was driving across town to meet Gary, Tom, and Pablo. "She Is So Deep" even came on a local radio station. My life had come a full, bizarre, happy circle.

"The plane ride here was crazy, Noah. Everyone was going ape-shit, drinking Bloody Marys and singing songs on the plane. Even the co-pilot seemed giddy," Agnes said, touching my leg a few times as she spoke, her voice full of passion and wonder. I was happy to see that whatever attraction we felt at Mike's funeral was still present between us.

"Yeah, the Saints just won the Super Bowl *and* it's Carnival," I said, navigating through the dense pre-parade traffic. "The whole city is in a fantastic mood."

"What actually happens during Mardi Gras, by the way? I've always wanted to know," she asked, her eyes fixed on all the revelers lining up on Saint Charles to watch Muses later that night.

"For about two weeks in February, these groups of people, called krewes, mask themselves and then ride in floats into downtown. People from every neighborhood come out and scream like crazies for plastic giveaways, called throws. Cops tell you to move back. Then marching bands pass by and scantily clad women dance."

"That's it?"

"Give or take a few beers, yeah."

She flashed me a disappointed look, asking, "So people don't have, like, crazy sex in the middle of the street?"

I laughed, my penis awakening again. "No, Mardi Gras isn't as wild as people think. It's more for kids."

"That's too bad," she said. I hung a right on Euterpe and got stuck in a slow-moving line of cars. "I take it you were hoping to see people fucking in the streets all weekend?" I asked her.

"I live in Dallas, Hollywood. Our neighborhood is so boring and orderly that I don't even think animals wouldn't fuck in public."

"And how is that going for you exactly?" I asked. I was ready to pull over and make out with her in my car.

"Do you mean my living in Dallas, or my marriage?"

"Both. I was asking about both."

"Roger's kids treat me like I'm the evil stepmom out of Cinderella. You'd think that they would give me a fucking break. I didn't make Roger leave their mom."

"That sucks. How old are they?"

"Leah's nine. Wendy's ten, about to be eleven."

"And how old is Roger?" I asked her.

"Seventy-five."

"No, seriously."

"Sixty-seven."

"Stop it. How old is he?"

"Forty-six, forty seven? Why?"

"Have you ever noticed the resemblance he has to Superman?"

"I don't think so, buddy."

"My dear, he looks just like Clark Kent."

"Well, he can't leap over tall buildings if that's what you're trying to say."

We were about a block away from the band's hotel by that point. The radio station was playing "Just Like Heaven" by The Cure, one of our favorites. Agnes turned it up.

"Is he coming to New Orleans this weekend?" I asked her, knowing that she was about to say *no*.

"We're not sure he can get someone to watch the kids. But to be honest I don't think he wants to come."

I asked her why.

"He's being a butt," she said, checking her iPhone. Then she read me a few of Superman's texts. Suddenly I felt anxious. Then she asked, "Will it be okay if I stay with you through the weekend if he can't make it? I can't find a hotel room anywhere. I tried."

"Sure," I said. "It's Mardi Gras. All the hotels were probably booked a year ago."

"I don't want to impose on you. Are you sure?"

You can impose your perfect little lithe nude body on me, I don't mind. "Will it be okay with Superman?" I asked her, smiling.

"Will it be okay with that girl of yours back at the school?" she responded. She was referring to Chloe, whom she had met at Randolph a few minutes earlier. When I introduced them in the faculty parking lot, Chloe kept giving me disapproving looks in regards to Agnes's everything—her leather skirt, her black fishnet stockings, her high heels, her obvious flirtations, as Agnes flung her arms around me and kept saying how wonderful I was.

When I rolled my eyes at Agnes, she said, "Yeah. She wants to fuck you, Noah. Fact."

"I don't think so."

"So, you're telling me you two haven't hooked up before? I'd like to hear you say it."

When I didn't say anything, she yelled, "I fucking knew it. *Look at you*, Hollywood! Not a bad catch there, but I didn't think you went for that preppy type."

"What do you mean *preppy*? You thought Chloe was preppy?"

"Hmmm. Let me see. The pearls. The tailored suit. Her boring schoolmarm attitude. I mean, *Little House on the Prairie* called and wants their clothes back."

I asked Agnes why she was jealous.

"I'm not jealous," she answered, laughing. "I know you still want me."

Once we got out of the car, Agnes came over to me, grabbed my hands, and said, "It's good to see you. Let's have a good time this weekend. I've missed you." And just like that I was back in the same place I used to be—in a state of wonder, lust, and devotion. *The same yet lovely curse.*

I had imagined a lot of scenarios, but I never thought that Gary's first words upon seeing me in New Orleans would be *Hi, Noah, sorry, but I can't do this.*

So my life *really* had come full circle—Agnes was flirting with me even though she was committed to someone else and Gary was threatening to walk out another door. *Bless my heart.*

It took a minute to figure out why Gary was pissed—he had just stormed out of a meeting in which Rudy Silverman and his producer informed him that our reunion gig needed to start at three in the afternoon on Saturday instead of at ten o'clock. They also said that we might have to play "She Is So Deep" as many as five or six times in a row so that the film crew could shoot us playing the song at every possible angle, essentially wiping out any chance at us having a genuine band performance that night. Finally, they wanted Gary, Tom, Pablo, and me to act out a few "pre-scripted scenes" that Rudy had written to incorporate into our episode.

"This isn't some kind of soap opera, buddy," Gary barked at Rudy after Agnes and I had corralled him back into the conference room where still everyone sat, waiting for us. I took an open seat next to Rudy and his Stooge, and gave a quick *what-the-fuck* glance to Tom and Pablo, who were sitting across the table from me with stunned looks on their faces. Maybe it was because Tom was so shocked, but he looked hollower than I had ever seen him, as though he were lacking vitamins or something. He just looked different. Pablo, though, looked the same as he always had, except for the million gray flecks now dotting his jet-black hair.

"I didn't come here to act for you guys," Gary barked behind his pair of Buddy Holly-style eyeglasses, which made him look fashionable as ever. He had become more muscular, too, I sensed, yet he was still very trim somehow—with two visible veins bulging in his neck as he sat eyeing Rudy and the Stooge, trying his best to remain calm.

"Let Rudy speak," Tom interrupted. It was beginning to dawn on me that our reunion show was in real jeopardy.

"Noah, hey, nice to see you again, and sorry for the confusion," Rudy said to me, "but my producer and I think that the show would be best served if certain scenes happened to be present in the episode—and certain dialogue, if you will."

"I don't understand what you guys are trying to do," Agnes answered, speaking up on our behalf. When Rudy gave her a *stay-out-of-this-bitch* look, I told him to back off because I had the same question. Finally the Stooge—the producer of *Bands Back Together*—chimed in, saying, "This is show business, fellas. This is what happens. We call the shots."

The Stooge was about fifty-five trying to look twenty-five, a total L.A. dick with a porn-star mustache that he fingered constantly. He also smelled of cheese.

Pablo rested his forehead on the table, in protest.

Tom started pulling his hair down over his eyes. He was still dreadlocked, of course, still skinny as shit. "What kind of scenes are you talking about?" I asked Rudy.

"Scenes I won't be in," Gary responded calmly, while checking his iPhone.

When Rudy started babbling about how each episode needed to follow a "certain dramatic formula," I quickly surmised that every *Bands Back Together* episode I had ever seen was most likely as scripted as *The Brady Bunch.* Rudy and the Stooge explained their *grand cinematic vision*—they wanted to film Gary and me taking separate cabs to Tipitina's on Saturday afternoon, both of us ranting about how we won't play the gig unless certain conditions are met. I would demand an apology from Gary for kicking me out of the band—and Gary, filmed in a separate cab, would insist that I admit that *Shebang* would have made a great album. All this bullshit would go on until Tom convinces us, backstage, our crowd cheering wildly, *that the show must go on because rock-n-roll will never die,* or something dumb like that. Then Gary and I would make up and hug each other before playing "She Is So Deep" fifty times in a row.

"That would be some episode, huh?" said the Stooge, smiling and stroking his mustache. The guy was getting creepier by the minute. "Especially if you guys say really inflammatory things about each other during the interviews," he continued.

"But we're already past that shit, man," Gary said, looking directly at me, interrupting him. "We don't feel that way anymore." I actually believed Gary was telling the truth. Something about him seemed different, on the inside.

"But it would be good television," Rudy said confidently, leaning forward and tapping his finger on the table. "You guys do your thing, and let us do ours. We got this."

"I don't understand. We're supposed to act like we haven't already agreed to play the show even though we have already agreed to play the show?" This was Pablo.

"Yep," brimmed Rudy.

Pablo continued, "You want us to act as though this moment, right now, isn't happening?"

"I can do it," replied Tom.

"Well, I can't," Gary quipped. "I came here to play a show with my friends, not be in some kind of falsity." I kept waiting for Gary to say that he needed to "live large," but he didn't.

"There's no way you should go on stage at three in the afternoon," Agnes told Gary, Tom, Pablo and me. "A Vows show isn't some kind of senior matinee. Am I right or am I right?"

"Look, we're just making recommendations," Rudy said, trying his best to appease us. "Nothing's set in stone, but we have to deliver twenty-two minutes of solid entertainment. Good conflict creates good television, right? That's TV 101. Haven't you seen our show before?"

He was talking to Gary, who simply shook his head *no*. The Stooge was starting to boil. "We never told you that your concert would start at ten o'clock," he said. "Tipitina's announced that, but they fucked up."

"We can't play to an empty house," Pablo responded. "No one will be there at three."

"We can arrange to get stand-ins," the Stooge said. "We've done that before."

I started to wonder when they were going to ask us to lip-sync the entire show, too. "What do you mean?" I asked. "Stand-ins?" Now I was beginning to get pissed off.

"We'll pay talent to show up. Don't worry about that," answered the Stooge.

"I'm not going to play a fake concert," Gary said.

"Hey, motherfuckers," the Scrooge finally erupted, his eyes becoming two small sideways slits on his tanned, greasy head as he screamed at us. "You guys signed a contract! Either you play at three, or you can eat a fucking lawsuit. Take your pick. I don't give a fuck."

Indie Darling

Then he and Rudy walked out, cell phones to their ears.

When Gary, Pablo, Agnes, Tom, Theresa, and I made it back to my house, we were all caught in the net of our collective depression. I considered hiding all the sharp objects in my kitchen because Tom was nearly on suicide watch, being so dejected that we might not play our show. Only Agnes was upbeat and garrulous, I remember, sitting flirtatiously on my lap, her inhibitions dulled by all the tequila she had consumed an hour earlier, when we all watched Muses pass a few blocks from my house, at the corner of Magazine and Upperline, where the purity of her marriage was also befouled. After catching a fistful of beads from a particularly generous float, Agnes came back to where I was standing, exalted, of course, and asked me to kiss her passionately, which I did. Except for a few raised eyebrows, no one in our group seemed to mind our coupling, save Theresa, Tom's wife, because she was the only one among us who had any stake in preserving the sanctity of marriage. I figured that Agnes would eventually sober up and stop being so affectionate with me (as was her custom), but when she kept whispering very provocative things in my ear as she sat on my lap in my living room, in front of everyone, it dawned on me that her Man of Steel, her husband Roger, might soon become a cuckold. The thought of him lingered in my living room like all the cigarette smoke trapped beneath the ceiling.

After Tom told us a miserable story about how he had recently been caught masturbating at work, Agnes said,

"Speaking of masturbating at work, Noah, tell us about that gal you're banging from your school. I think the guys would like to know that you're dating a Miss Priss."

"You're banging a student?" Tom asked excitedly, the perv.

"No, she's over thirty and we're not dating. Agnes is just jealous," I said playfully, remembering that Chloe had asked me to give her a call that night. She hoped that she and her friends could watch the parade with us.

"Am not," Agnes replied, sticking her tongue out at me. I watched Gary in the corner of my room, eyeing my book collection. He was picking up his old copy of *Thus Spoke Zarathustra*, which I kept somehow but never read. No one in our group could put his or her finger on it exactly, but Gary Davis Gary *did* seem different now, less intense and quieter. It was the conversation we all had, behind his back. Tom even said that Gary had asked him not to call him Gary Davis Gary anymore. He was now, according to Tom, only Gary Davis.

"Agnes, how's married life?" Theresa interrupted, eyeing Agnes's hand on my thigh.

"Show us a photograph of her pearls, Noah," Agnes said, ignoring Theresa's question and referring to Chloe again. I wanted to change the conversation. "Tom, tell us another one of your stories. Didn't you tell me that you got punched by a cop a few years ago?"

"That guy was a fucking asshole," he said, rolling a joint. "But I don't want to talk about it right now."

Agnes, being more adept at group conversation, asked everyone to name the weirdest thing that had happened to us since we last saw each other.

When no one volunteered anything, Agnes yelled, "I got fucking married! Ha!"

"Can you believe that nonsense? The agony of it all," I said playfully.

"Cheers," she said, before raising her wine glass to her lips.

"I went to India," Gary offered, still lingering in the corner, in the periphery.

"Did anyone recognize you there?" Agnes interrupted. "You know, you and your famous locks?"

"Not really," he answered, stifling a laugh, which prompted Tom, for some reason, to recount one of his favorite Vows stories—the night in Boston when Gary got attacked by a horde of teenage girls who wanted him to sign their panties. But when the last one revealed that she wasn't wearing any, Gary signed his name across her belly. "I thought you were going to sign her ass, man. That's what she wanted you to do," Tom laughed. "I still have photos of all that badassery."

"What's it like being a teacher?" asked Gary, picking up my Fender acoustic and playing a bluesy chord progression in the vein of The White Stripes. As I gave him my rote answer, I couldn't help but consider what riff I would play over Gary's chord progression, nearly wishing that Agnes would get off my lap so that I could pick up my other guitar and go play with him.

Tom finally asked what everyone in the room wanted to know. "Gary, is that song yours?"

"I wrote it a few weeks ago, yeah," he said demurely, avoiding eye contact with us while re-tuning the pesky high E string of my guitar. Pablo, meanwhile, had already picked up my old bass and was looking for a cable. Tom, his head as though on a swivel, asked me if I had a snare drum around. It seemed like we were all about to play. "No, sorry," I answered him.

"Tune this much, Noah?" Pablo asked, referring to the bass guitar that was now slung across his body.

"Go on, honey," Agnes said, nudging me towards my guitars in the corner. She knew me well.

It only took a few minutes for us to do what we did best. I came up with a decent riff to Gary's chord progression, playing a variation of the melody Gary was humming. Then it was Pablo, I think, who came up with the change for the chorus. Agnes, in typical helpful fashion, came back from the kitchen with a few pans for Tom to bang on so that he could join in. After we had the melody, chorus, and bridge down, Gary asked me for a line to sing in the song's chorus. I answered immediately, *the more things change the more they stay the same*, because it had been stuck in my head the whole day. When Gary wanted another line to conclude the chorus, I added, without much thought, *what little we learn we learn a little too late*.

And that's how the song came to be. After playing it, from start to finish, a few times, we made a rough recording of it in

Garage Band, although the mix was awful, because Tom was too close to the mic. He was smacking my pots like a crazy person. Afterward, we all sat around serene and relaxed, with the glow of lovers post-sex. I definitely exhaled. Then *inhaled*.

Tom, of course, had rolled the fattest joint. Feeling exalted, I guess, I took a few hits off it, to everyone's surprise. A few minutes later, I knew I was stoned when I kept repeating to everyone that I could climb the Empire State Building "just like King Kong."

Just like King Kong, I kept saying.

At first I thought it was only a paranoia-based hallucination of the little fucker—because I had heard that he had been shipped off to Vermont already—but I opened the front door and saw him standing there in his red hoodie. He smirked.

"How long have you been here, Miles." I was afraid that he might have seen me smoking Tom's weed.

"Long enough to know that the song you guys wrote is damn good. You should let me release it on Bandcamp, tonight."

I stood there, stupefied by the long scarf of frosted breath emanating from my mouth. It looked like crystal stars were pouring from my head whenever I breathed.

"You are stoned, Mr. Seymour!"

"Am not," I answered, closing my mouth and turning off my star-machine.

"Uh, newsflash, sir, yes you are," he said, imitating the stern tone I often used to address him. I felt a sudden knot in my stomach. "Do your parents know that you're here?" I asked, knowing that his mom would shit her panties if she knew that Miles had reappeared on my porch.

"Are you asking me if I am a missing person again?"

"Don't fuck around. I can lose my job."

"Everything's cool, Mr. Seymour. My parents are on a ski trip. My sister is watching me."

"I thought you were in military school already, in Vermont."

"My mom and I just went up there to check it out. I'm going back in a few weeks. Something about a block system or something?"

Then Agnes came out on the porch, took one look at Miles shivering in the cold, and escorted him inside. Tom thought he was the pizza deliveryman. "Hey dude, where's our pie?" he kept asking him, twisting and pulling his dreads down in front of his eyes.

"What pie?" Miles answered back, annoyed.

"Our fucking pizza, little guy," Tom repeated.

"Why would I have a pizza?"

"Do you have our pizza?"

This went on for a while. It was like watching two monkeys try to fuck a football.

"Everyone, this is Miles Lafayette," I interrupted. "He used to be a student at the school where I teach, but he got himself kicked out. For doing something really stupid."

I think someone clapped for him.

"But he can't stay. He's about to leave. Aren't you, Miles?"

When I turned to escort him out, Miles had already gone over to introduce himself to Gary, who was at my refrigerator, looking at some photographs.

"Do you like to party, little guy?" Tom asked Miles from across the room, offering him his newly rolled joint.

"Tom, don't. Fuck!" I exclaimed. "He's only fifteen years old."

"Sixteen," Miles replied, walking towards Tom.

"Miles, if you touch that thing, I'll kill you."

At some point I drowsed off because I was suddenly aware that the group was in the middle of a heated conversation about *Bands Back Together*.

"I know, but I don't want to play under all those conditions," Gary told Tom calmly, showing his newfound reserve of tranquility. "I won't enjoy the show, doing it their way. Their whole enterprise is a joke. Can't you see that?"

"Come on. Let's do it for Mike," Tom begged, pulling the dead-bassist card. "We have to at least play the show for Mike."

"Mike would have never played at three in the afternoon," Pablo laughed, crossing himself and then pointing upwards to the sky.

Then Miles asked, "Why don't you guys just play somewhere else, like at a smaller club or something? Tip's is bourgeois anyway."

I was happy because he didn't seem to be stoned.

"Well, our show is booked at Tip's," Tom answered him matter-of-factly, as though Miles were really stupid.

"I know that, dude," Miles responded. "Just screw that shit-show and play somewhere else."

I chimed in, having woken fully from my marijuana-induced nap. "Well, we don't have the equipment to play anywhere else. *Bands Back Together* was going to supply us with most everything we needed, and I'm damn sure they aren't going to let us borrow any of it so that we can play somewhere else."

"I can round up gear for you. My band has everything," Miles said. "My bassist's dad owns a music store out in Kenner."

"How cute," Agnes said, sitting next to me.

"He's right," Gary said confidently. "We should just play somewhere else, somewhere more low-key and less bourgeois."

So they *were* the same person. Miles was just Gary Davis Gary at fifteen.

"You have, like, a drum set I could play?" Tom asked Miles, not quite believing him. "Like a *real* drum set?"

"Uh, the *drummer* in my band does," he said sarcastically, making everyone laugh. He had really become the life of the party. I wondered why I couldn't stand him sometimes, when other people seemed to like him so much.

"What's the name of your band, Miles?" Agnes asked.

"Indie Darling," he answered, giving me an eat-shit look.

"That's what they used to call me," Agnes answered.

"Me too," Gary laughed.

"If we don't play Tip's, where will we play?" Tom asked, his stupid mouth full of cold pizza as he spoke. Agnes chimed in. "You guys are the fucking Vows. What club wouldn't have you?" But Tom was right. Every club would have been booked months ago, given that it was Mardi Gras weekend. "Finding a suitable place to play might be impossible," I said.

Gary and Miles rolled their eyes at the same time.

"And how will anyone know that we're playing somewhere else?" Tom asked. "Everyone is going to show up at Tip's, right?"

"Do you mean at three in the afternoon?" Pablo asked sarcastically.

That's really the last thing I remember before I woke up again, probably an hour later, with my head cradled in Agnes's lap. I asked her where everyone had gone, because my apartment was cleared out. I looked at my phone to check the time, and saw that Chloe had called twice without leaving a message. My mouth was full of cotton.

"They all left, baby," she said, looking down at me and tracing a delicate line on my chest with her finger. Two forked veins were visible on her forehead like a snake's tongue. I looked around the room again.

"Where's Weebly?" I asked her, sitting up.

"Who's Weebly?"

"The kid. Miles."

"They took him home. Tom took your car."

"Jesus Christ."

Then Agnes silenced me with a soft kiss, her mouth recently freshened by cold water and toothpaste. After she whispered into my ear, I took her hand and followed her into my bedroom, where she wanted me. Afterward, we tried to stay awake to see the sunrise, but we fell asleep in each other's arms before the light replaced the dark.

Track Twelve

The next morning I was strutting down a surprisingly sunny Magazine Street in my old jeans, a T-shirt that read "I Have a Black Belt in Crazy," a pinstriped charcoal-grey vest, and a scuffed pair of black Doc Martins adorned with gold laces, an homage to my friend Jen from college. All I was missing, I remember thinking, was my pack of Camels in my left shirt pocket, but I had given up smoking for good. In my old garb that morning, I felt reborn and free, albeit a little silly, and I told Gary as much after I spied him in a corner table at Rue, a *New Yorker* folded in his hands, and a faint mustache of milk on his upper lip.

"I haven't worn these clothes in years," I said, looking down at my old belt buckle with a Fender Telecaster emblazoned across it.

"Your pants do look a little small, yeah," he replied, smiling.

Gary, however, still owned his natural rock-star look, donning a dark-blue Western cowboy shirt with small white paisleys, corduroy pants, and a hemp necklace tied around his muscled neck. His hair was a wavy, tousled mess of freedom that morning, and his three-day stubble lent his chiseled face an air of carelessness. I was happy to see that he still seemed to be the Gary from the night before—calm and tranquil. "What do you wear when you're teaching?" he asked me, his milk mustache from his latte now gone.

"You know. Dress shirt. Slacks. Noose around my neck," I said.

"Get out of here."

"Seriously, they hand out nooses at the door when you arrive in the morning," I said, looking around to see if anyone from Randolph was within earshot. That Friday was a holiday for everyone—students, faculty, and staff.

It felt good to make Gary laugh. Even though we didn't get a chance to sit down the night before and talk privately, I felt we had gotten along fairly well, considering the odd circumstances of the evening. Perhaps it was because we had a common enemy now—Rudy and the Stooge—but it also seemed like Gary had made a valiant effort to make me feel at ease around him. It was time to bury the hatchet. "So, are we good now?" I eventually asked him, my hands flat on the table.

"I hope so. I regret all that shit, from the past. I look back and realize how stupid and selfish I was. I was carrying around so much anger. I'm really sorry."

I oversimplified my reply, answering, "I'm good, too. I'm over it. I apologize as well." A silence ensued, as though we realized our conversation had too many parts to it and had thus become too heavy to lift. "You definitely seem more chill now," I eventually said.

"That's what everyone says."

I spied a few girls, twenty-something, sitting stiffly in a corner booth, their eyes transfixed on Gary. I had forgotten what it was like to be out in public with him. I made the vague head motion I used to make back when we were in The Vows, the one that let him know *people are staring at you, dude.*

Gary continued, unfazed, "It's cliché, but I went to India. I got clean, started practicing yoga. Self-realization. I'm closer to my dharma now."

"Was that in English?" I asked him, trying to make a joke. Part of me was skeptical that his whole yoga/self-realization thing was just another Bob Dylan-inspired spiritual phase that wouldn't last.

"I know. I'm weird." He changed the subject. "New Orleans seems cool, huh? Very different vibe than L.A."

He pulled out a little piece of scrap paper from his wallet and showed me what he had found earlier that morning and had written down—*New Orleans is a town of transients and vagabonds, a city that welcomes them with open arms. If the Statue of Liberty were at the port of New Orleans, the famous poem would read, 'Give me your drunk, your poor, your huddled masses yearning to break free of their past and become someone new.'*

"Ha, that's about right," I told him, forgiving his interest in the old cliché about New Orleans. "Where did you find that?"

"In that paper over there," he said, pointing to our local weekly.

"*The Gumbo*," I told him.

"Yeah, there's a nice article in it about us. Have you read it?"

"Yep."

The article that Gary was speaking about was a profile about The Vows, which was inspired, I guess, by our upcoming show at Tip's. The article made me blush, actually, because the writer kept saying very congratulatory things about us. It was obvious that the writer liked the band, *a lot.*

"Is it always like this?" he asked, gesturing towards a frenzied Magazine Street, referring to the palpable energy in the city.

"Not really," I said. "It's Carnival season, *and* the Saints just won the Super Bowl. It's like a perfect storm of parties."

"What a fucking game, huh?" he asked, referring to the Saints' comeback victory over the Colts. I told him that I was too busy grading essays to watch it. He also knew I wasn't too much of a football fan.

"How much is rent here? For your place, I mean?" he asked.

"About a thousand a month."

"That's not bad."

"Why? Are you thinking of moving out here?" I asked him, laughing.

"L.A. is getting old. I'm not really feeling it anymore."

"All the botox?" I asked, being stupid.

"Yeah, that's part of it."

"Didn't I read somewhere that you started a new band? How's that going?"

"It fell apart like a chair," he said matter-of-factly. Then we shared our own horror stories of trying to start bands since The Vows dissolved. Gary spoke of one guy who keyed his car after he told him that he wasn't good enough to be in a band, with anybody. After I told him about my weird experience at Mike's funeral, the subject of Tom came up.

"That guy is doomed to terminal adolescence," Gary said, shielding his eyes from the sunlight that had begun pouring through the window. "He hasn't changed at all."

"I think his marriage is doomed, too," I replied, referring to a conversation I had had with Tom the night before, the one in which he told me that he wanted to hook up with somebody after Saturday night's show.

"Everyone needs to chill with their midlife crises," Gary said.

"What do you mean?"

"You and Agnes?" he said, smiling.

"I know. Didn't see that one coming." I wasn't really ready to talk about her with him, so I changed the conversation. "Hey, did Miles get home safely last night?"

"I like that kid," he answered.

"You mean you like the kid *who got home safely last night?*"

"Yeah, we dropped him off. He was fine."

"Dropped him off where?"

"At his house."

"Were his parents there?"

"Why all the questions?"

"Sorry, long story. I'm trying to make sure he isn't lying to me. I could get in trouble at work."

"You can see for yourself. We're supposed to go back to his house later today to check out his band's equipment. We might need it tomorrow night."

Now I really need Miles's parents to be out of town, I told myself. "So you guys decided, then? We're gonna try to play somewhere else?" I asked him calmly, trying to make it clear that I wouldn't be upset if the band had made the decision without me.

"No, but I know how I feel," he said before pausing. "Rudy and that dude can eat a bowl of dicks."

"A bowl of what?"

"Dicks."

"You sound like Miles."

"I like that kid."

Track Thirteen

Carnival season, for me, has always been a take-it-or-leave-it sort of affair, but later that night, watching Agnes, Tom, Theresa, Pablo, and Gary run alongside parade floats with the enthusiasm of children made me feel relaxed and happy, too. We found a festive corner at Seventh and Saint Charles, a few blocks away from Miles's parents' house, where we could witness the majestic krewes of Hermes and Morpheus. The weather that night was perfect—sixty-two degrees of warm humid Southern air and a transcendent yellow moon suspended in the trees above us. Even the azaleas on the neutral ground were beginning to open, mocking Louisiana's winter.

We had, however, made little progress that afternoon at finding a new place to play. Every club was completely booked, of course. One Eyed Jacks wouldn't even listen to us, thinking that we were trying to pull some kind of prank on them. In fact, by the time we set out for Miles's house that night, only one decent-sized club had offered us a stage—some out-of-the-way joint near the Jefferson Parish line that mostly booked cover bands, but Gary nixed the idea of playing there when he saw their horrible website and awful gas-station décor.

So when the parades passed us and we started walking over to Miles's house, we were beginning to think that our best option might be to play the *Bands Back Together* gig after all. We had convinced Condon to negotiate on our behalf, and he quickly scored two victories for us—we wouldn't have to do any of Rudy's phony-ass interviews before our show, and we wouldn't have to start at three o'clock either. But Gary didn't trust that Rudy and the Stooge wouldn't try to pull some sneaky shit on us at the last minute, so he wasn't convinced.

Tom's mood had definitely improved since the night before. "How do you live here with all these gorgeous black women," he asked me excitedly, still ecstatic from the tumult of the parades and the marching bands and the helicopters making their dramatic noise overhead. "I've had the biggest hard-on since I landed at the airport yesterday," I remember him saying.

I couldn't decide if Tom's constant sexual talk was just his shallow way of trying to relate to me, us being men, but he made it seem like he wanted to bang every black woman he saw. Between Tom's desire for infidelity and Agnes's real infidelity, the weekend was turning out to be anything but a heady thumbs-up for the covenant of marriage. In fact, Agnes was even *sans* wedding ring by that point, I remember, having placed it on my dresser before we left for the parades. I saw it sparkle right after I turned off the lights and closed the door.

"I guess there are no black women in Seattle?" I asked him, feigning interest in his rampant sexual desire because, truth be told, I was more interested in talking about where we were going to play the following night. I was trying to stay calm, but my patience was wearing thin. "Dude, we have a total dearth of the black hotties up there," Tom replied.

"Wow, that's amazing," I answered, but Tom wasn't the best at detecting sarcasm.

"You're sitting on a little treasure of big black beautiful African-American women here, Noah. New Orleans is the world's capitol of bilfs."

"Bilfs?" I repeated, needing clarification, but then I figured out what he was saying, so I stopped him from explaining. "Why don't you move here then?" I interrupted, semi-toying with him.

"We're talking about it. Theresa has family in Alexandria, you know? Just look at that ass," he exclaimed, pointing to a woman across the street carrying two balloons and a fistful of cotton candy.

"Whatever blows your hair black, I guess," I answered him, my pun intended. Tom thought that was just the funniest thing ever, so he put his arm around me as we got nearer to Miles's house and asked, "So I heard you and Gary kissed and made up today?"

"Who told you that?"

"The one and only Gary Davis Gary. Wait, I mean Gary Davis. Shit."

"I guess you could say that we made up, yeah. It was nice actually," I responded.

"Did he really apologize to you? Did he actually use the words *I'm sorry?*"

"I don't have it on tape or anything, but I think he did."
Then Tom took a deep breath and looked around, surveying
the scene, before saying, "I never thought I'd live to see this
day, Noah. Us hanging out and shit. Even Gary told me that
he's having fun here."

"Gary used the word *fun?*"

"I know. I nearly slapped him. He says he's changed
now, though. Yoga this. Yoga that. *Fuck.* I even think the
asshole went to an ashram this morning. I saw him in
the hotel lobby with a yoga mat. I told him he's probably
menstruating."

Laughing, I turned around to see Gary, who was walking a few feet behind us with a Mardi Gras mask on his face,
partially to preserve his own anonymity and partially because
he was caught up in the Carnival atmosphere. He was talking demonstratively to Pablo and Theresa about something,
pounding his fist on his own chest as he spoke. Agnes was
walking behind them, talking on the phone with Maya, the
Autumn Set's multi-instrumentalist, and trying to convince
her to get on the first flight to New Orleans. Maya was also a
teacher now, in Houston.

"So what's up with you and Agnes?" Tom asked, punching me playfully on the shoulder and smiling devilishly. "You
guys can't keep your paws off each other."

"I don't know what you're talking about."

"What do you mean *you don't know?* You fucking know,
you horn dog."

"I'm just as surprised as you are, to be honest. Maybe
she's just inspired by Mardi Gras?"

"Is she going to leave her husband, or is she just fucking you for the weekend?"

"We haven't fucked." I was lying to him, of course.

"Yet," he said.

"I don't know what's going to happen."

"And that's killing you, I bet."

It was, in fact, killing me—the *not knowing*, even though I denied it to Tom. Agnes and I had spent the entire afternoon together, but we didn't have one of our famous, stressful "discuss the relationship" talks, in which I'd push Agnes to commit to me and she'd back off from an inability to do so. I was trying my best to just be in the moment, as Gary would later advise, but I was anxious and contemplative.

When we finally got to Miles's house, the huge gate at the sidewalk was open. "Jesus, these people are loaded," Tom blurted, referring to the gargantuan size of Miles's house—a three-story imposing Victorian mansion with intricate gables, wrought-iron work, and cupolas.

"Does Edgar Allen Poe live here?" Pablo asked.

I didn't want to be there, obviously, so I was lingering behind the group. They had made their way to the front door, searching for the doorbell.

"I have to pee so badly," Agnes said, squeezing her thighs together playfully. "Just knock on the motherfucker already."

Gary knocked. Then we waited. No one answered. My intuition told me that no one was home. Eventually Pablo said with a wry smile, "I think I heard someone say *come in*. Did you guys hear it too?"

"No, I didn't hear anything," Tom answered, not realizing that Pablo was only looking for an excuse to enter the house. Before Theresa could finish a sentence, Gary had already opened the front door and had walked through the foyer of the mansion. Only when Agnes turned around and begged me to come inside, so that she could use the bathroom, did I relent and cross the threshold myself. Miles's house bled even more wealth than it did from the outside, with its thirty foot high ceilings, intricate crown molding, gold this, gold that, leopard print everywhere, antique everything, spiral stair-cases leading to the upper part of the Earth's atmosphere. The entire living room looked like a museum in which no one had touched anything for years. Nothing was out of place. *No wonder Miles was always trying to break out of here*, I thought to myself.

"Hello, little guy?" shouted Tom, having forgotten Miles's name. Then he turned to me. "What's the fucking kid's name?"

"Miles," I whispered.

"Miles!" Tom screamed. "Miles! Hello?"

I still had my hand on the crystal doorknob. I was trans-fixed by the large portrait of Miles's mother, Gail, hanging in the foyer. In it, she looked about twenty years younger, although as repressed, cynical, and bitchy as ever. Her stern elongated nose was set like an arrow pointing toward the front door beside me, through which I wanted to bolt. "Maybe we should go," I offered. "I don't think anyone's here." I felt the familiar malaise in my stomach.

"But I need to pee so badly," Agnes implored.

"No, we need to go, come on."

"I'll be right back," she said, before disappearing around the corner.

"We should go," I whispered to the group.

"We can't leave Agnes here," Theresa said, frowning. Tom had seen me staring at the painting of Miles's mom, so he came over to examine it, too. "Looks like something very large is stuck up her ass," he said.

"You have no idea," I answered him, whispering. "That's Miles's mom, Gail. She thinks I'm corrupting her son."

"You probably are," Tom said. "Just like you're corrupting Agnes's vagina."

I gave him the finger.

Then Pablo warned that someone was approaching the front door. My first inclination was to hide, so I told everyone to duck behind the couch in the living room. But because Tom and I were still by the front door, we slid behind a tall, heavy window curtain.

What happened next was bizarre and comical, something straight out of a bad teen movie. A plump college-age girl and a drunk-as-balls frat guy barged through the door and began to make out, feverishly, on the couch behind which Theresa, Gary, and Pablo hid. Of course, Tom started to ogle at them from behind our curtain, trying not to bust up. Seconds later, via certain hand gestures, he let me know that Miles's sister had started to give the guy head, even mouthing the words *shock and awe* to me.

When Agnes finally came back from the bathroom, completely unaware of the lovebirds on the couch, she asked Pablo, Theresa, and Gary, sort of loudly, "Why are you guys on the fucking floor?"

I swear to you that the girl screamed louder than I had heard anyone scream in my life. "What the fuck are you doing here, bitch!" she kept repeating.

"Um, hi," I said nervously, stepping out from behind the curtain, like I was some kind of game-show host asshole. "I'm Mr. Seymour."

"Get the fuck out of here!" the girl barked loudly, eventually noticing Gary, Pablo, and Theresa behind the couch. I think she thought that we were some kind of home invaders.

"I'm Miles's teacher from Randolph Academy. Mr. Seymour?"

Luckily, Miles came into the room to see what the commotion was about. He had been in his room upstairs, listening to music on his headphones. "Hey, guys, who screamed?" he asked us calmly, not fazed at all that we were all standing in his living room. It became clear that the plump girl was Miles's sister. "Miles," she asked him sternly, "do you know these people?"

"Yeah, Lauren, they're the fucking Vows."

"Hi," Tom said, going over to go shake her hand stupidly.

"Get the fuck away from me," she told him.

"Lauren, don't be such a bitch," Miles said.

"She isn't being a bitch, Miles. We scared her," I said.

Then Lauren's boyfriend smiled and asked, "You guys are The Vows, really? That's cool." He had already zipped up his pants and was no longer embarrassed. He had so many fucking Mardi Gras beads around his neck.

Eventually our apologies were accepted, heart rates fell back to normal, and Miles led us to the garage apartment in his backyard so that we could check out his band's equipment in case we needed it for the following night. Tom, of course, immediately told Miles that his sister had been giving her frat boyfriend head.

"Shut the fuck up, man," Miles responded. "Not cool."

Then Tom started impersonating Lauren giving a blowjob. I asked Miles if his parents were, in fact, out of town. "Yes, they always bolt for Mardi Gras. They don't like black people walking around their neighborhood."

"That's racist," Tom said.

"Jesus, what is this, Versailles?" Agnes asked to no one in particular, as we made our way through Miles's backyard, which was dotted with moss-draped oak trees, majestic light installations, towering water fountains, shrubs cut in the shapes of animals, and statues of Greek gods.

"This should really be called a *grounds*, not a backyard," Tom said, sounding a little snobbish.

"You sound like my father," Miles replied to him, who flipped his red hood to cover his head.

It turned out that Miles's garage apartment was loaded with very expensive musical equipment. Tom immediately went over to the drum set in the corner, a vintage Ludwig maple-shell five-piece, and slammed down on the snare drum, hard. Then I remembered why I was nearly deaf in my left ear—because I always stood with that ear closest to Tom's kit, both on-stage and during practice sessions. "Hello, deafness, my old friend," I said out loud—my old catchphrase to let Tom know that he should play a little quieter. "Can I adjust your snare, to make it a little tighter?" Tom asked Miles.

"That's what she said," Pablo quipped.

"The kit has good tone," Tom said. "Is your band any good?"

"Why don't you ask this guy right here?" Miles answered, pointing to me.

"Yeah, they're *very* good actually," I said, lying, of course.

Tom asked Miles if his band had a record deal.

Miles laughed. "It's not the 90's anymore. You don't need those people. We release our own shit, whenever we want," he answered.

Tom rolled his eyes.

Gary was having trouble finding the on-button to his keyboard—some Yamaha super-conductor that looked like it cost around a million dollars. "How do you turn this thing on, Miles?" he asked, setting his Mardi Gras mask on top of it.

"Just hit the middle C," Miles said.

When Gary struck the key, very dramatically, the instrument lit up and sounded a long, drawn-out harmonic eighth. "That's pretty fucking cool," Gary said.

"Are we, like, going to play right now?" I asked the group, although by the time I finished my question, I already knew the answer based upon everyone's body language. Meanwhile, Miles's sister, Lauren, and her boyfriend had entered the room to see what was going on. Tom, upon seeing them, started humming 70's style porn-film music while drumming along to it.

"Stop, you're such a dick," Gary said, while looking at a blushing Lauren.

"I'd like to go over a few of the songs I'm not totally sure about. I don't want to get up on-stage tomorrow night without rehearsing them once," Pablo said.

The knot in my stomach had grown bigger. Agnes called out, "Play 'Ton of Love,'" which, ironically, was a song I had written about her. Then Tom asked the dreaded question. "Are we going to play any of Gary's *Shebang* songs tomorrow night?"

I looked over at Gary.

"No, I think those songs are dead," Gary uttered calmly, messing around with his new keyboard. I noticed a framed Vows poster in the far corner, one of my favorites, the one that had The Vows written in *The Godfather* movie style, with the drawn hand beside it, holding the puppet strings and everything.

"Gary, I'm cool with it. We can play your songs," I told him. I guess I was inspired by the fraternity of the weekend.

"No, let's just play *The Weary Boys* in its entirety, from beginning to end. Plus any covers that we can still remember," he said, laughing. The whole weekend was turning into a dream come true, I told myself, save for the *Bands Back Together* fiasco.

"'Brown Sugar?'" Tom blurted out quickly, winking at me.

"Not a chance," I replied. "Sorry."

"What about your new one from last night?" Miles asked us. "Play that song."

"Yeah, we could work that one up so that we could play something new tomorrow."

This was Gary, of course.

"Right now?" I asked. *Some things never do change*, I guess.

"Which song?" Tom asked, stretching his wrists again. He had a very particular routine before he started playing the drums. First he stretched his back, then his neck and shoulders, before finally contorting his wrists backward.

"Never mind," Gary replied.

"The whole Nirvana album?" Tom asked.

"Jesus, Tom."

"What in the fuck are you guys talking about?" Agnes asked.

"Let's start with something I kind of already know," Pablo finally demanded. "How about 'She Is So Deep' for old-time's sake?"

I watched Gary nod without complaint.

Everyone looked at me because I was the one who started the song with my intro riff. But I started off in the wrong key and had to do it again, trying to stifle an embarrassed smile. Then we proceeded to sound like total high-school amateurs. Tom was dragging at times, late on some of his fills, and Pablo, understandably, was having trouble playing Mike's more complicated bass lines. Not to be outdone, though, Gary was flat in the high ranges, especially during the dramatic, concluding chorus of "I Want to Die In San

Francisco," one of our signature moments, so he had to slip into falsetto at times. As for my own playing, I wasn't stinking it up as much as the others, but Miles's blue Danelectro kept going out of tune on me and didn't have the tone I wanted. I had also quickly developed one bitch of a blister on my left index finger, so I wasn't exactly nailing my solos. By the time we set our instruments down after thirty minutes of rehearsing, we tried to act all cool, but our faces betrayed our defeat. Only Miles was cheery, standing there, having danced his ass off the whole time, drenched in his own victorious, self-driven sweat.

Track Fourteen

Later that evening, having just exited a random second line in the Marigny, we all agreed to scrap the whole *Bands Back Together* idea and instead play at a small bar in the French Quarter, NOLA Apothecary, which we had dropped in on earlier. When Pablo told the bar's owners that we were looking for a new venue, they literally begged us to perform there, proclaiming that they were great admirers of the band. Finally, it was Gary who convinced us that an intimate show at a very small bar would be better than a fake televised one at a legendary club.

"Come on, T, change those things on your dogs already and get a move on.'"

This was Tom, urging Theresa to change the Band-Aids on her feet more quickly so that we could catch the end of DJ Hot Feet's set at Mimi's. Our whole caravan, *sans* Miles—I was able to ditch him in the French Quarter—had stopped on the neutral ground at Elysian Fields and Royal so that Theresa could attend to her blisters. It was Theresa, in fact, who had begged us to leave the second line moments earlier, even though everyone else was having a blast.

When she finally stood up, ready to continue walking, Tom cheered sarcastically. Meanwhile, Gary was on the phone with the owners of NOLA Apothecary, informing them that we would take them up on their offer of hosting the band the following night.

I watched him converse, silhouetted by a warm radiant moon. "Thank you, so much," he said. "Yes, we will do so. Around 8ish for the sound check? Noah? 8 o'clock?"

He was looking at me. I gave him a thumb's up.

"Yes, around eight, for the sound check. No, it will be our pleasure," he continued. "Absolutely. Tell her hello. Yes. Whatever you want. No, we got everything. Okay, see you tomorrow. That was Tom. Sorry. Bye."

When he hung up, he told us, very dramatically, that he couldn't wait for our show.

"Bullshit, honey. You just want to go back to that place so you can tap that bartender's ass."

This was Agnes, referring to the tall and gorgeous female bartender at NOLA Apothecary whom Gary had been flirting with the whole time we were there. Since no one had actually seen Gary *flirt* before (normally he acted so blasé around women, letting them come to him), we stood there stunned, mouths open, like dumbfounded tourists standing before the amazing new monument of Gary Davis Gary. "It was rather nicely shaped," Tom said, referring to the bartender's ass and ignoring Theresa's eyes of scorn.

"Tell me you at least got her number, Gary. Please," Agnes said.

"Of course, I did," he responded, putting away his iPhone, cool as ever.

"No one has anything on your ass, baby," I told Agnes, taking her hand. I was leading the way.

"That's what she said," Tom replied instantly, trying to be funny but failing.

"What's her story?" Pablo asked Gary. "She seemed pretty cool."

"She's a dancer. Does yoga. Had no idea who I was. Wants to be an actress. Sofia."

I could hear the second line up ahead. Costumed revelers were darting this way and that, laughing and dancing, as if spelled by the fat moon and all the celebratory vibes. "I need to start doing yoga," Agnes interjected. "Just look at my ass."

"We all do," said Gary.

"Excuse me?" Agnes said, laughing.

"I mean, *we all need to do yoga*," Gary clarified.

"On your ass," Tom blurted. Theresa hit him on the shoulder. I started to feel bad for her, because she was limping.

"Can we fit all of Miles's shit in that place?" Pablo asked us, changing the conversation back to our gig the following night. "That bar was pretty fucking small."

"Do they even book bands there?" Agnes asked, reading my mind.

They were looking at me. "I doubt it," I said.

"We will rock that shit," Gary answered. "Don't worry about it."

"Think of it this way. We might not want a big crowd, considering how badly we sounded earlier," Tom joked.

"You're the one who couldn't keep a fucking beat," Pablo replied.

"Oh yeah, you shit fucker? You sounded *worse* than someone who had never played the bass before. You sounded like Noah."

As we got closer to the second line, it crossed my mind that we had finally come full circle as a band. We were four guys again, without a record contract, excited to play at some hole-in-the-wall with nothing to lose. We were out late, being adventurous and free. It was my imagined life, part two. Although Mike's death was unfortunate, yes, his absence seemed to create a new harmony between the four of us. Or maybe it was just our inevitable maturity as adults that brought us some peace? I couldn't decide, and neither did it matter. I opened the door to Mimi's and bought everyone a round. *Was my happiness dependent upon being in a band?*

After Theresa, Tom, and Pablo returned to their hotel around four in the morning, Gary, Agnes, and I found ourselves in the backseat of a cab, headed back to the French Quarter so that Gary could get a Tarot reading. With the windows rolled down and some warm humid air in our faces, Agnes returned to a conversation we had shelved earlier. "Seriously, though, Gary, what the fuck?" she asked, putting on a new coat of cherry-red lipstick.

But Gary didn't know what she was talking about.

"You're so chill now, like a different person," Agnes continued.

"You think so?"

I nodded in agreement, lifting my go-cup and saying *cheers*. "What the fuck happened to you?" Agnes asked playfully.

"It's cliché. I warn you," Gary responded.

"I won't judge," Agnes interrupted him. "I drive a mini-van and watch Roger's kids play soccer. I think I can handle clichés."

"Do you remember how I used to love being in storms and watching bad weather?" Gary asked her. "No, what kind of storms?" Agnes answered.

But I remembered. Whenever we were on tour, Gary loved driving straight into bad weather. The bigger the storm, the happier he was. One night in Oklahoma, to everyone's disbelief, he made our bus driver pull over in the middle of a huge lightning storm so that he could run out into the thunder and the tumult—with nothing but his underwear and boots on. I just figured that he was high as fuck again.

"When I was traveling in India, there was this huge typhoon approaching the village I had been living in," he said. "Wait, when was this?" Agnes interrupted. We were stopped in traffic, I remember. There was some kind of commotion going on at Royal and Dauphine—a kid being arrested.

"About three years after the band broke up. 2004, I think. The typhoon came right over us; it was the most intense storm I had ever seen. Trees were laying horizontal, or snapped in two. Roofs were flying off buildings. And in the middle of all that shit, I crawled outside onto a pier, on my knees, not even able to stand up. I was just getting pummeled by the wind and rain."

Even the cab driver had turned down his radio so that he could listen.

"Then all of a sudden I got knocked in the water, as though the pier had collapsed or something. I couldn't see much, but I could feel myself getting pulled farther out."

"Uh, death-wish, you think?" Agnes asked him.

"I thought, *This is it. I'm going to die. This was my life.* So I called out to a god, anything."

"And then Jesus came to you on a boat and saved your famous ass?" Agnes asked him playfully. "No, seriously," Gary said. "Seconds after I called out, I felt my body being rushed back through the water, very quickly, like I was in some kind of suction. Then all of a sudden I was back on the pier, on my belly, alone."

"Shut the front door," Agnes said.

"Maybe it was a backwash wave, I don't know," Gary answered calmly. "But ever since then, I've been clean. With this peace inside. It felt like—"

"Like what?" Agnes prodded him.

"Like everything is going to be okay. All the time."

"Namaste," I said, joking. I didn't really know what to say.

"I had been living the wrong way, carrying around such destructive energy," Gary continued.

"Like that typhoon," Agnes said.

"I hadn't thought of it that way, but I guess you're right."

The first person I saw when I stepped out of the cab was Sofia, the gorgeous bartender from NOLA Apothecary, whom Gary must've invited to meet us. "Hi, I'm Noah. We met earlier," I said, extending my hand to her as Agnes and Gary remained in the car, paying the cab driver. I noticed that she was Gary's type to a T—long straight black hair, pale skin, blue eyes, slender, shy, probably wrote poetry. "Gary asked me to meet you guys here. What is this place?" she joked, looking up at the neon-lit sign that read HAUNTED TOURS AND TAROT NEW ORLEANS. "Normally I avoid Bourbon like it's the plague," she continued.

"Yeah, me too. But, you know?" I said, pointing over to Agnes and Gary, insinuating that they were tourists, technically.

"Hey, Sofia." This was Gary, swooping in and relieving me. They kissed each other politely on the cheek. "You've met Noah. And this is Agnes, his lover."

"What's up, buttercup?" Agnes asked Sofia, trailing her into the voodoo shop on Bourbon. "Your ass is thriller."

After an awkward wait in the lobby, Agnes convinced me to get a reading of my own. We were directed to follow a trail of what looked like bird seed to a dark room in the back to meet my fortuneteller, Paul, who, once we got near the door, asked us in a deep voice to come in and sit down. It was hard to see anything, especially the chair on which the dude kept asking me to sit, on account of all the darkness. I felt nervous for some reason. Agnes took a seat behind me, where I couldn't see her face. "A palm reading will tell you what you already know about yourself. A Tarot reading will tell you about your future. Cost is the same for both," Paul said, waiting for my answer. It looked like he was sitting in a wheelchair, I couldn't really tell. There might have been a cat on his lap, too, or a ferret? Maybe a dead mongoose?

I turned around to look at Agnes. When she didn't say anything, I shrugged and chose the Tarot card reading. Then Paul splayed his huge deck of cards on the desk in front of me and asked me to pick two. I chose what felt to be the first and the last card in the pile. "Hmmm, this is interesting," Paul said, scanning my cards with his flashlight. "The Death card and The Hanged Man."

"Is there, um, like, a light in here?" I said.

"Relax. The Death card isn't as bad as it seems. It suggests more of a transformation than a physical death. You're in a period of deep change in your life right now, correct?"

"Uh, yeah," I said. "I just became a teacher."

"And what did you do before that?"

"I played music."

"Well, the Death card suggests that the people and things you counted on in the past may no longer be available to you in quite the same way. This transition can be difficult. So take care in determining what you become so that your renewal is a positive one."

"Bingo!" Agnes chimed in behind me, all bright and cheery.

"Let's consider the other card, The Hanged Man. Paired with Death, this card tells me that you're definitely at some kind of crossroads in your life, a time of deep reflection and possibility of change. You're thinking of either jumping in, or jumping out. Digging in or moving on. Does this resonate with you?"

I was freaked out because the characters illustrated on both cards looked dead. "I don't understand. It looks like that dude's dead, too," I said nervously, referring to the man hanging upside down on one of my cards. Paul shone his light on it more fully. "I don't see him as being dead, just suspended. Maybe you're stuck like him, suspended between two things, wondering whether or not you should be a teacher or a musician? Be alone or committed…to something?"

I swallowed hard, attempting to make the dry knot in my throat go away. Paul, sensing my stress, continued, "This card may also be telling you to shed any self-limiting beliefs. Be very careful about what you think, especially about yourself, as you can only become what your mind tells you that you are."

"Got it. Is that it?" I said. I was ready to bolt. After shuffling the cards again, he said, "Let's look at your love life. Pick two cards again." Agnes coughed comically. I drew the Hermit Reversed. And, once again, the Death card. Agnes, unable to see my cards, asked, "What is it?"

I hung my head. Paul spoke up. "The Hermit Reversed is an interesting card for you. In terms of your love life, it suggests that a romance from your past might be re-kindled. Someone whom you loved long ago might come back into your life."

Agnes giggled. *The same yet lovely curse*, I thought to myself. I could feel my face getting hotter. Paul continued, "But you should ask yourself whether that is really what you want.

Once again, a crossroads. Your cards are very clear. You're very lucky. This is a good reading. Many people's cards can be unclear."

I'm pretty sure I stood up to leave, immediately, without even asking if my reading was over. "Good luck, my friend," Paul called out to me as we left him in the darkness of his dank room, in a wheelchair, perhaps, with an animal on his lap.

Once we left that weirdness and were out in the lighted street again, Agnes calmed me down and helped me laugh it all off. She was patting my head softly, imitating a mother's tenderness, when I read Gary's text saying that he and Sofia had bailed already. It was five in the morning. I hailed another cab and watched Agnes fall asleep with her head on my lap. With my hand running through her hair, I felt a final straightening of the crumpled love we had kept for one another. After many years, it seemed, she and I were beginning to unfold. I carried her in my arms, like a prince would, from the cab to my front door so that she wouldn't have to touch her feet to the ground. But when I pushed open my gate, it wasn't Miles I saw, but Roger, her husband, who was waiting for us on my porch.

Track Fifteen

Her marriage was over.

Roger could see it in her eyes, her unfaithfulness. I didn't hear the entire conversation between them, but I know he told her *that his daughters deserved someone better than a mom who still didn't know who she was and who forsook all of her responsibilities to revisit her glory days as a musician.* He called her a tramp and a slut and stormed off, leaving her in a wake of confusion, tears, and doubt.

I let her sleep in my bed, alone, to give her some space, while I drowsed on the sleeper sofa in the spare bedroom. When I woke and heard her blowing her nose around four in the afternoon, I checked on her. "It's cold in here," she said, as I turned up the heat. From the look on her face, it seemed like all the intimacy we had woven in the past few days was about to unravel. I sat down beside her, ready to hear about how sorry she was for messing around with me when she was in another relationship. I knew what she was about to say, word for word. "You're probably, like, holy shit. What a fucking mess, huh?" she asked me.

"You mean about Roger?" I asked meekly.

She sat up. Her eyes were puffy from crying. I had seen those puffy eyes before.

"Yeah."

"How did he know where I live?"

"I was thinking maybe I should go home?" she asked, tracing unintelligible shapes on her knee with her finger. "I don't know what to do."

I told her that it wasn't my decision.

"I'd like to know how you feel, though," she said, lowering her eyes from mine and putting her necklace into her mouth, one of her signature gestures whenever she was contemplating something. To be honest, I had been thinking, ever since Roger left, that I shouldn't have gotten involved with someone's wife, even if it was Agnes. My mind spied ahead, and I saw a fate similar to Gatsby's. A cursed future, a cursed bed. "I don't want the same thing to happen to me again," I told her.

"And what's that?" she responded, growing irritated. It was like she *wanted* to be mad at me.

"I don't want to fight with you."

"Neither do I."

My phone started to ring.

"I don't want to be your rebound guy."

I had been waiting years to say those words, I think.

"So you think you're just some kind of rebound guy to me? Great." She started tracing shapes on her knee again.

"I don't know what I am to you actually. You've never told me."

My phone kept ringing and ringing. Whoever was calling kept hanging up and calling me back after getting my voicemail. "Maybe you should answer that," Agnes said, dismissing me. She was making it seem like removing the loose strand of hair on her shoulder was the most important thing in her life.

It was Gary. "Sorry to keep bombing you with calls," he said, a little breathlessly. "Are you there? Noah? Hello?"

I had been watching Agnes get up and walk five feet to the bathroom and close the door.

"Sorry. No worries. What's up?" I asked him.

"Can you drive me to the airport to get Condon? I don't want him paying for cabs."

We had all pitched in the day before, to fly Condon down to New Orleans so that he could watch our reunion show in person—and to buffer us from any unforeseen threats from Rudy and the Stooge.

"Sure," I said, remembering that I had told Gary I'd do so. "When does his flight get in?"

"About five minutes ago."

"Fuck," I said, unable to hide my stress.

"How long does it take to get to the airport from here?" he asked.

"About forty-five minutes."

"Fuck," he said, mocking me.

From the sound of it, Agnes had started herself a bath—or maybe she was just letting the water run in the tub endlessly, I couldn't tell. I didn't want to leave, but at the same time I didn't want to keep Gary and Condon waiting. Over the din of the rushing water, I tapped on the door and told

Agnes that I'd be back in a few minutes. I waited for her reply, but she never said anything.

Luckily I was able to navigate around the street closings in my neighborhood, but when it took longer to get to the Warehouse District than I thought, my heart started beating irregularly, *fluttering like a trapped bird*, I remember saying to myself, melodramatically. When I finally pulled up in front of Gary's hotel, I saw him arguing with Rudy Silverman behind the revolving glass doors, just inside the lobby, chopping his hand in front of Rudy's chest, as if to dramatically make some point. When I honked, Gary came spilling out with Rudy following him. Once Gary got in the car and closed the door in Rudy's face, my phone started ringing again. I was hoping it was Agnes. It was Chloe. I let her go to voicemail. "What does that asshole want?" I asked Gary, referring to Rudy, whom I was watching getting smaller in my rearview mirror.

"Our souls."

"Tom's is for sale, I think."

"Well, mine's not."

He took a deep breath.

"Did you tell him about NOLA Apothecary?" I asked.

"Fuck no."

"So he thinks we're still playing at Tip's?"

"He can eat my balls, man."

We spied Condon by the curb at the airport, a stout, lonely, and bearded creature amidst a flock of other badly dressed tourists who had flown in for the debauchery of Mardi Gras. Immediately I could tell that time hadn't done him any favors. Condon's belly, which had always been quite large, was protruding outward even farther than before, and his eyes had become more wrinkled, as if all he had done since I saw him last was stand squinting into the sun. I placed his bags into my trunk and then felt the weight of his heavy hand shaking mine. "Good to see you, Hollywood," he said, smiling his big toothy grin behind his messy full beard. "Is that Gary Fucking Gary in your front seat?"

"In the flesh. Sure as shit."

"Well, goddamn. Never thought I'd see the day. Both you and him in the same fuckin' car. This calls for a celebration! Did you bring me a drink?"

"Ha, no. What do you think this is?"

"New Orleans."

Admittedly I am not the best at staying in touch with people, so I had to catch up on Condon's life, post-Vows. He was still in the music business, he said, now a talent scout for Impact Records. He had managed a few other bands after our demise, but they never made it. "It's all changed, man," he waxed sadly in the backseat of my Volvo. "Radio determines everything now, not talent. A record company won't wait three minutes for a band to develop and find their shit. They'll give a band, like, *two weeks* to break. Fuck, I don't think anyone would sign The Beatles today. And worse yet, no one buys records anymore, so the only way you're gonna make money is by touring, which has also turned into a fuckbag. It's a goddamn wasteland out there now, brothers. Be glad you're out of the shit show."

"Yeah, definitely," Gary said absently, not really interested in Condon's stories. He was texting Sofia, his bartender friend from NOLA Apothecary. The gigantic hickey on his neck, strangely in the shape of Japan, told me that things had gone well for him the night before. "I guess that little hickey of yours means that you and Sofia…?"

I finished my sentence with a raised eyebrow and a crude hand gesture.

"Not cool, man," Gary said, feigning anger and rolling his eyes at me.

"Same old Gary Davis Gary, banging the chicks, huh?" Condon blurted from the backseat, where had taken out his flask and had begun taking large swills of his scotch.

"Hey, Condon," I told him. "It's just Gary Davis now. You're looking at a new man. Isn't he, Gary? Go on, tell him."

It felt good to tease Gary, actually.

"Noah is banging Agnes again, by the way," Gary responded dryly, trying to get back at me. "Thought you should know."

"Shit, nothing has changed at all. Gary's banging groupies and you're still worshipping Agnes's trick pussy."

"Except Mike is dead," I said, trying to be funny but falling short. There was an awkward silence.

"I'm sure you're happy about that shit, huh, Noah?" Condon finally asked before ejaculating his big obnoxious laugh. Everything about Condon was big, in fact. It was as if he had swallowed Texas on his way over and might eat through half of New Orleans during his stay. I looked at him in the rearview mirror. We smirked.

"Poor Mike," Gary said. "Let him be. May his soul rest in peace."

When Gary answered a call from Tom, I relayed the silly plot line of the past few days to Condon. I told him about our first fucked-up meeting with Rudy and the Stooge, about Agnes's surprise arrival, about Tom and Theresa's constant bickering, and about Miles, who, according to Tom, was on his way to Tip's at that very moment to inform about fifty of our fans that we would be playing at NOLA Apothecary. I didn't tell Gary or Condon, of course, the part about Roger showing up on my porch. I wasn't ready to talk to anyone about Agnes and me yet, to be honest. My heart fluttered again as we dropped Condon off at his hotel in Metairie.

Gary and I had been listening to Spoon's new album, *Transference*, in silence for a while, before he asked me a question. "Did what I say last night freak you out?" he muttered, turning down my car's stereo. "When you said what?" I asked back. I wasn't sure what conversation he was referring to.

"The huge storm in India? Going out on the pier like a stupid fuck. Nearly dying?"

"Oh, yeah," I answered. "No, that didn't freak me out. Why?"

It had started to drizzle outside, prompting a few revelers to cross Poydras stupidly, nearly getting themselves flattened. I thought of Mike's head flying off his body.

"I haven't told anyone this, but I'm pretty sure I was trying to kill myself that night. I mean, I never really admitted it to myself," he said, his voice trailing off. "But I knew what I was doing. I had been pretty fucked up for a while, you know? I know you do. And then it got worse in India because no one knew who I was. So I could obliterate myself even more, using things I couldn't control."

My phone started ringing again. Finally, it was Agnes. My heart did its thing.

"So you were trying to drown yourself, you think?" I asked distractedly, reaching down to silence my phone.

"Yeah. Pretty fucked up, huh?"

I didn't know what to say. "Jesus, Gary. Do you feel better now?"

"Yeah, completely. That's what I was trying to tell you and Agnes last night. I'm focusing more on living in the present now, because that's all there really is. Trying to keep it light, you know?"

I was contemplating Gary's words as I pulled up to his hotel. I'm pretty sure I had my own necklace inside my mouth, imitating Agnes's contemplative gesture. The attendant in the hotel's loading zone kept motioning me to drive off, getting all fucking crazy and making me even more nervous. I finally felt ready to tell Gary about Agnes and me—and about Roger showing up that morning—but instead I asked him how things were going between him and Sofia. Gary unrolled the window and calmly asked the parking-attendant guy if we could have a few more seconds. "She's awesome, man. Very serious girl. But I barely know her."

I looked at the Japan-shaped hickey on his neck and wondered if he would move to New Orleans to be with her.

"I'm glad you didn't die, Gary," I finally told him, finding the words.

"Me too. Or else you wouldn't be here right now," he said jokingly, getting out of my car. "I'll see you in a little bit for sound check. Should be an interesting night, huh?"

Watching him disappear into the swarm of people in his hotel lobby, I realized that I was finally seeing Gary clearly for the first time in my life. He was no longer false and fucked up and belligerent and self-destructive. He was no longer bent on *living large*, nor was he in some kind of a bullshit Bob Dylan-inspired phase. He was himself now—quieter, more true and vulnerable.

Then I wondered how I had grown in the past decade—or if I had grown at all.

Pulling away, I listened to my voicemails—one from Chloe and one from Agnes. Chloe, sounding tipsy on a parade route somewhere, screamed into the phone that she was excited to see our show later that night. She sounded flirtatious again. Agnes, in a long message full of familiar silences, said that she had just booked a flight home and was in a cab on her way to the airport. She also declared that she was *sorry*. *And that she loved me*. I listened to her say those words again, three times in a row, before I deleted her message. Then the questions started flooding in. *Was I supposed to make a set list? What song should we open with? What song should we close with? Should we play "She Is So Deep" in the beginning, middle, or end of the show? Were we supposed to have a mailing list for our audience? Would I remember all the chord changes of the songs we might play? Would the blister on my finger pop during our show? Did Agnes really love me?*

Then came the flutter, again, of my heart.

When I got back to my darkened house, I had about five minutes to shower, change my clothes, nibble on something, and pack all my shit into my car before heading back to the Quarter for our sound check. But from my kitchen, where I was drinking a glass of water, I saw someone lying in my bed.

Track Sixteen

"**W**hat are you doing here?" I asked her, my body leaning against the doorframe at the outer edge of my bedroom. "I thought you were on a plane."

"Come here. Keep the light off. Hurry." *So much for concentrating on our show*, I thought to myself, as I climbed into bed with her. I didn't even take off my shoes.

I could tell that she was no longer mad at me.

"Noah."

"Yes, Agnes," I answered.

"That preppy lady from your school came by."

"Here? When?"

"Right after you left."

"Okay. What did you tell her?"

"I don't want to leave."

"You told her that you didn't want to leave?"

"No, I'm telling *you* that. Screw her."

"I see." I paused. I was going to be late for our sound check. "You said you loved me, Agnes. On the phone."

"I did?"

"Do you mean it?"

"Yes."

I was beginning to get hard. Her body against mine was so warm. I pressed against her.

"I don't want to share you with anyone anymore," I said.

"What do you mean?"

"I don't want to wonder when you're going to go back to Roger, or anyone else. I don't want to be the guy you think you love but—"

"Do you love me?" she interrupted.

"Yes, I do. But—"

Then she kissed me, slowly at first, before biting my lip, knowing that kissing me in that way turned me on. Then we became this hot mess on my bed, pushing and pulling and driving into each other, as though we were trying to erase the invisible line that existed between us, between all lovers, which had kept us separate. When we came at the same time, a few minutes later, we collapsed into each other's arms, exasperated, unraveled.

"No one has ever made love to me like that," she said, tucking in strands of sweat-soaked hair behind her left ear. For once, I didn't feel empty. "Good," I said, wondering if she and I were at the beginning of something, or at our final, dramatic end.

I couldn't really enjoy my grand entrance into NOLA Apothecary because immediately after entering the side door on Toulouse, Agnes and I were accosted by a very pissed off Chloe in leather pants and a tight-fitting Rolling Stones t-shirt (the one with the open mouth and tongue on it). She started yelling at me because Miles was there, with the band, drinking a beer and helping everyone set up.

"Great, and I can see you're screwing your ex now, too," Chloe continued, referring to Agnes, who had just blown cigarette smoke in her face. "Thanks a lot."

"This doesn't concern you," Agnes replied, putting her arm around me.

"Aren't you, like, *married?*" Chloe answered her.

When I didn't say or do anything, Chloe continued, "Maybe you don't care anymore, Noah, but I'm *this* close to calling the cops and having someone's ass thrown in OPP for contributing to the delinquency of a minor. Please go get that beer out of Miles's hand. He's in a vulnerable place right now."

"I'll take care of it," I said to her calmly. "I'm sure it was all a misunderstanding."

"A misunderstanding? Really?" She had her hands on her leather-wrapped hips.

"I said I will take care of it."

"When are you going to grow up?" she asked me, before storming off. Her exit left a vacancy inside, or her words did.

"Forget her. She's not your type," Agnes said, squeezing my hand. "Plus, I think she has a dick."

"Well, her dick is going to get me fired tomorrow. I'm sure of it."

As we inched our way through the crowded bar, I spied our instruments perfectly arranged on a stage riser that Tom and Pablo had bought that afternoon. It was enough,

I think, to stop the irregular beating of my heart because I don't remember my melodramatic *damaged bird* fluttering again after that point. With all the craziness of the weekend, I wanted to disappear into the sweet oblivion that only music could offer me, and I was trying to convey that feeling in words to Agnes when we finally found Gary, Tom, Theresa, Pablo, Miles, and Condon in a small private office at the back of the bar. Everyone, including Miles, was surprisingly upbeat, happy, and *sober*. Gone, evidently, were the days when Mike, Gary, and Tom would get smashed before we took the stage. I stood there smiling before my big, crazy, immature family—a family I knew I missed, even though they were standing right in front of me. "Asshole, you're lucky that Miles can play all our shit," Tom barked at me from across the office, feigning anger at my having missed our sound check. "I think you have some competition now, buddy. I'd watch your ass. The kid made us sound better than you did last night."

I walked over to Miles and grabbed the beer from his hand. It was empty anyway. "I know," I replied. "I'm sorry I missed our sound check. Traffic is insane right now. It's Endymion Saturday. Parades."

"Bullshit, we see your bed hair," Pablo answered, insinuating that Agnes and I were late because we were having sex. I blushed.

There were a few conversations going on, I could tell. In one corner of the office, Pablo was conveying to Gary and Theresa how much he had enjoyed being in the French Quarter earlier that afternoon, listening to brass bands and soaking up the festive atmosphere of the city. A few feet away, Miles was detailing his experience at Tip's earlier, when he was there handing out flyers to a few of our fans, letting them know that we were playing at NOLA Apothecary instead. But when a crew member of *Bands Back Together* got his hands on one, Miles recounted, Rudy and the Stooge went all ape shit and accosted him in the street, firing a million questions at him. "What did you do?" Agnes asked, wide-eyed.

"I told them to eat a bowl of dicks," Miles answered confidently, earning a big-bellied laugh from Condon. "They just kept screaming at me, especially the weird dude with the mustache."

"The Stooge!" Tom yelled from across the room, earning another chuckle from the group. Damn, we were all in a good mood. "Did anyone get the Stooge's name, by the way?" Agnes joked, handing me her beer to taste.

"Theodore?" Theresa guessed.

"Everard?" Pablo answered.

"Willard?" Gary replied.

"Dick Odor?" Tom said.

There was a knock on the door. Sofia the bartender poked her beautiful head in. "Hey guys," she said meekly, not wanting to disturb our camaraderie. "How many people did you let know you were playing here tonight?"

"Why, baby?" Gary asked her.

Gary called her *baby*. How cute.

Then she opened the door behind her, more fully, so that we could see how packed the place had become. It looked like three hundred people had crammed themselves into a space that could fit only forty. We all looked over at Miles. "Um, Miles, how many flyers did you hand out today?" I asked him.

"About a hundred. I also posted it on Facebook."

"Why did you do that?" I asked him.

"I didn't know your show was some kind of secret, Hollywood."

"Don't call me that."

"Shock and awe, man," Tom said, beginning to stretch his wrists in anticipation of playing.

"We need an opening band," Gary said quickly, anticipating how impatient the crowd could become. We didn't want to go on-stage for another hour or so.

"Agnes, will you play a few songs to hold them over?" I asked her, laying on the charm. I think I was even batting my eyelashes.

"I'm not fucking Joni Mitchell," she quipped. "I'm not going out there alone."

"Miles, why don't you play something?" Gary asked him.

Then Miles grabbed the guitar next to him and started playing the intro riff to Jimi Hendrix's "Purple Haze." I might have been the only one who knew he was doing it sarcastically. "Wait, is this kid any good?" Condon asked, fulfilling his old role as the learned manager of the band. Despite his large belly and historical scotch consumption, Condon still harbored good managerial instincts. He knew that it would be a bad idea to put a shitty musician, especially a teenage kid, in front of a large, expectant crowd. "I can play, boss," Miles answered him quickly. "But can we get the rest of my band in here to play with me? They're all outside, actually. They can't get in."

"Why didn't you guys put his band on the guest list?" Agnes asked us.

"This is a *bar*," I answered. "They have, like, homework and shit."

"How is *he* in here then?" Theresa asked, pointing to Miles.

"This guy was helping us load our equipment," Tom said. "No one said anything."

"Well, Miss Sorensen did," I said to Miles dryly. He rolled his eyes. Agnes squeezed him.

"I'm pretty sure we can let his band in to play," Sofia said. "But you guys need to be responsible for them."

About thirty minutes later, Indie Darling took the stage in front of a swollen, expectant, yet polite crowd. Even though their drummer was a little overmatched, Miles was completely unafraid as a front man, maintaining eye contact with the crowd and gyrating his hips a little as he sang. Indie Darling wasn't that bad. I wouldn't call it a prayer exactly, but I remember wishing—to something, the universe, I guess— that Miles's experience of being a musician—*his own same but lovely curse*—would fare better than mine—and Gary's.

I whispered to Pablo that Miles's band was a cross between "The Pixies and—"

"The Vows," he said quickly, cutting me off. He was right. They did sound like us. Gary leaned over to ask if he could see the set list I had made. "Oh, shit," I told him, freezing for a moment. "Don't tell me you didn't make a set list, Hollywood," he joked.

"Do you have, like, a fever or something?" Pablo said, touching my forehead. "Tom bet that you would have made around fifty of them. One for each of your moods or whatever."

"I have an idea," I told them, listening to Miles dedicate his last song to Chloe, who had been shooting me evil glares throughout Indie Darling's set, her arms wrapped tightly around her chest. "Tell everyone to meet me back in the office."

Track Seventeen

I grabbed some paper napkins from the bar and headed back to the office where the band was waiting. "Listen up, everyone," I commanded. "Here's what I need you to do."

Everyone fell silent, except for Tom, who kept talking to Sofia.

"Tom, shut the fuck up, man," Condon told him.

"Why do you guys always have to stomp on my dick?" he responded.

I gave Tom, Gary, and Pablo a cocktail napkin and told them to tear it into four pieces. Then I directed them to write down, on each scrap, the name of a song they wanted to play that night. They could pick four songs total. Afterwards, I explained, I would put all the torn scraps of paper into a hat and then pull them out randomly, creating our set list for the night.

"Wait, you only gave me one napkin," Tom said, still talking to Sofia.

"Yes, dick head," Condon said to him.

"So I need to write my four songs on one napkin?" Tom asked, getting defensive.

"Tear it up into four pieces and then—"

"Why only four songs?" Tom interrupted. "I want to play more than four songs."

"Here, let me help you," Agnes told him, taking his napkin.

"Covers, too? Can we write down covers?" Pablo asked.

I hadn't thought about that. "Guys," I asked, "should we play any cover songs?"

"Sure, why not?" Gary answered.

When Condon heard that we hadn't practiced much, he went into full protective mode, suggesting that we should play our easiest-to-play songs first. "Yeah, but I'm thinking we should embrace the dangerous, what-the-fuck element of this show." This was Pablo, laid back as ever. "It's only rock-n-roll, right?" he said sarcastically.

"But I like it," Agnes said, continuing the joke.

I wrote down my four songs: "She Is So Deep" (because I feared that no one else would write it down); "I Want to Die in San Francisco"; "Magnolia"; and Blondie's "Heart of Glass" (because I knew Agnes would have to get on-stage and sing it for us). After I put everyone's scraps of paper into my hat, I asked Condon to write down the names of the songs in the order in which I called them out.

"This is fucking crazy," Tom said, but I knew he loved the excitement of it.

"It has a certain shock-and-awe element to it, I know," I answered him, teasing him. I drew our first number, "What Little We Learn We Learn a Little Too Late," the song we wrote at my house on Thursday night. My stomach sank because I wasn't totally sure I remembered all its changes. "What fucking song is that," Condon asked me, shaking his head. He didn't like what we were doing.

"We wrote it two days ago," Pablo answered confidently, making me think it was he who had selected it.

"Is it any good?" Condon asked.

"Best song ever, man," Pablo said.

"And you're going to open up the show with it?" Condon asked skeptically. Then he made a farting noise with his mouth. "Best song ever, man," I repeated, doing my best imitation of Pablo.

"Maybe you guys should re-think this," Condon offered.

"I Want to Die in San Francisco," I called out, cutting him off and declaring our second song. I watched Condon write it down, shaking his head.

"She Is So Deep."

"Fuck!" Gary blurted, laughing. "I was hoping no one would write that song down."

"Uh, sorry, darling," I said. "It just had to be done."

"What happens if we all write the same song down? Do we play it four times? I don't understand," Tom asked. I wanted to hit him in the head.

Then I pulled "Just Like Heaven" by The Cure. I could tell it was Tom's choice, based on his handwriting. Plus, he loved playing that song. "I don't think I remember all the words," Gary said.

"I do," Miles said eagerly, who had just come into the office room after finishing his set, to everyone's applause.

Then he started singing the lyrics to "Just Like Heaven" and impersonating Robert Smith's honeyed voice. "I guess you're getting up on stage to sing it with me then," Gary replied, earning a bit of laughter.

"Are you serious?" Agnes asked.

Gary answered *yes.*

"No way, bitches! I want to sing and play with you guys, too!" Agnes complained. "I mean, if that's cool with y'all."

Then, as fate would have it, after I called out Neil Young's "Hey Hey My My," I pulled Blondie's "Heart of Glass."

"Oh, fuck yeah," Agnes said, knowing that it was I who chose that song so that she could sing it for us. "I love you, Noah," she said.

"Get a room," Tom said.

"Get a divorce," I whispered to him.

"We sure are playing a lot of covers real quick," Condon said, still on protective mode. "Maybe you guys should play some originals too?"

I think we all answered *no* in total syncopation, total harmony. We hadn't had this much unity in the band in, well, forever. "What's next?" asked Pablo.

"Wait until you pull my songs," Tom said, twisting his dreads down in front of his eyes.

Then I called out "Extended Drum Solo."

"Tom!" Theresa exclaimed.

"Your wet dream has come true, Tom. Congrats." This was Agnes.

"How long can you go for?" Pablo asked him.

"That's what she said," Tom answered. I'm pretty sure the whole room groaned.

"No more than two minutes, right, Theresa?" I asked her.

"That's what she said," Agnes answered. More groans.

"Three minutes tops. Maybe four," Tom replied.

Then I pulled a number of Vows' songs: "Dizzy," "Magnolia," and "Ton of Love." Condon looked relieved.

"The set list has now become boring and suspect," Gary said afterward. "We need to fuck things up. Here, let me pick." I passed him the hat, and he spied into it before carefully choosing a scrap. "Read this one," he said, handing his choice to me.

"My Rock-n-Roll Fantasy?" I said, reading Gary's chicken-scratch handwriting.

"I'm not playing any Foghat songs," Tom barked.

"It's not Foghat. It's Bad Company," Pablo answered.

"No, men. I meant The Kinks' version," Gary offered.

But I didn't know how to play it. I didn't know it.

"I don't think we've ever played that song together," Pablo said.

Tom consented, a unified front.

"Can I play it by myself then, on piano?" Gary asked. "I mean, if Tom gets to play a five-minute drum solo, then why can't I play one song by myself?"

"Hello, solo career," Agnes joked.

But no one seemed to mind.

Agnes asked how many songs we had drawn, and Condon answered *thirteen* without a beat. After some discussion, we agreed that we needed to play about fifteen to seventeen songs, choosing to keep our set on the short side in case we sounded like shit. I unfolded Gary's next song, Dylan's "Tangled Up in Blue."

"Did you even write down any The Vows' songs?" Pablo asked him playfully, saying his attempt to become Bob Dylan was nearly complete. "I was hoping we could play it as an encore, please," Gary said, ignoring Pablo's question. "We've always done a good job on that song, our slower version. Do you guys remember it?"

When Agnes added that the song had a Louisiana/New Orleans connection, I agreed with Gary. We would close the show with it. I was done arguing about set lists, or trying to control the band. "I'm not sure you'll be asked to play any encores, seeing as how this set list is shaping up," Condon joked. "Maybe you shouldn't count on playing any encores."

"We're going to rock this shit," Gary answered. "Next song." Then I drew a few more Vows' songs, including "Oceanside for Shelley." After I pulled the last piece of napkin, I was nervous yet excited about going onstage. We were definitely taking some risks with the set list.

When everyone fell into his pre-show routine, Tom came over to me, saying, "Gary said that you and Agnes went to a palm reader last night? How was that shit?"

"It was creepy. The guy kept saying stuff like my past was coming back around full circle and that I needed to make a choice between my future and past self. Shit like that. It was like he *knew*. I was kind of weirded out. It also looked like he had a dead animal on his lap."

"That's freaky *Thriller* shit, man," Tom answered. "I went to a psychic four years ago, on my thirty-sixth birthday, and he told me that Theresa and I would be divorced in five years."

"What do you think about that?" I asked him.

"Sounds about right."

Moments before going on-stage, Miles asked Tom, Gary, Pablo, and me to huddle together for a photo. After some initial resistance, we eventually lined up as we normally did—with Gary in the middle, Tom to his right, Pablo to Gary's left, and me next to Pablo. It was then that Theresa mentioned that it was strange not seeing Mike with us, who normally stood next to Gary. We all sort of fell silent for a moment, thinking of him, until Pablo joked, "That dude sure liked to lift weights."

"And do push-ups," Tom said.

"And be fucking pissed off at me," I joked.

"You guys should dedicate tonight's show to him," Theresa said with tears streaming down her face, having become emotional all of a sudden, she said, from seeing the four of us stand together, with Mike missing. When Condon, Miles, Agnes, and Theresa started snapping photos of us on their iPhones, my questions started flooding in again. *Would we even stay in touch after tonight? Would Agnes and I last? Did we have what keeps two lovers together? And weren't Tom and Theresa approaching a divorce, just like Agnes and Roger were? And wasn't Chloe evaluating Miles because of a screenplay he wrote about a kid who kept driving his car off the Mississippi River Bridge? Was he suicidal, just like Gary was? Were we all falling apart?*

But in my mind, in that moment, I didn't want to have any more questions. I wanted to grow as a person, as Gary had grown. *Why don't you feel lighter, Noah? Isn't life extraordinary? Come on! Grow! Don't moments of happiness exist, like this one? Can't you feel it, how people or events can resonate inside your chest like music does, to make a beautiful, dying strain?*

Tom whispered to me, "Don't go into one of your voids, Noah."

"Life is complicated, Tom," I replied, my own tears about to fall.

"Let it go," he said, putting his arm around me.

And I tried to let it go—my thoughts, my worries, my sense of self in the larger world. I remembered what Chloe said to me that night on our date, *No one knows what will happen, Noah, ever.*

Moments later, we walked onstage, one after the other, like The Beatles on the cover of *Abbey Road*, I thought. The crowd's ovation was like an ocean swell lifting our spirits. With my Telecaster firmly across my chest, I spied Agnes at the side, standing beside a beaming Miles, who was filming us with his iPhone. I looked over at Gary, who was adjusting his microphone stand and staring blankly into the audience, cool and composed as ever. Tom played a quick, meaningless fill on his drums, and Pablo made final adjustments to his bass. "Check, check," Gary said dutifully, monotonously. Then a lone spotlight found Gary at the center of the stage, illuminating him in a warm bath of radiance. Very quietly he leaned forward and said, "We are The Vows," and I hit the loud, ringing, heaven-and-hell notifying E chord, which threw on the light we balanced above us in the vaulted and mystical universe.

Bonus Track

"Heard in New Orleans: The Vows at NOLA Apothecary,"
Tim Quigley, *The Gumbo*, Monday, February 15, 2010

I'll admit it. I'm pretty skeptical of all the bands reuniting these days, whether it's Pavement or The Police. Too often the attempts "to get the band back together" feel like a desperate money grab, cheapening each band's triumphant return. Or it's like watching your grandparents dance—you love them and all, but that doesn't mean you want to see them on-stage any more.

When I heard rumors that one of my favorite bands from the early 2000's, The Vows, was slotted to play a reunion gig at Tipitina's, I felt exhilarated yet fearful. Exhilarated because The Vows have always been a great live act, yet fearful because I didn't want my memories of them spoiled. We tend to glorify the dead, and The Vows had already taken supreme reign in my mind and memory, exactly where I wanted them to be.

It turns out that I had nothing to be afraid of. The Vows' show on Saturday night was one of the best—and curious—concerts I have been to in a long time. To begin with, there was a chaotic last-minute venue change. For weeks The Vows' show had been billed at

Indie Darling

Tipitina's, but right before I entered the doors at Tip's, a teenage kid named Miles Lafayette (more about him later) pulled me aside to tell me that The Vows were playing, instead, at a small bar in the French Quarter. When an unnamed friend of mine who works the bar at Tip's told me that The Vows never made their sound check that afternoon, I made some phone calls and found out that the kid's story was legit: The Vows were playing somewhere else. The Tipitina's show, I knew, was one of those "Bands Back Together" televised performances that you might have witnessed in horror in the privacy of your own home, but the band decided to scrap playing in front of television cameras and play instead at NOLA Apothecary. Yes, that's right, NOLA Apothecary—the new bar on Toulouse that can fit forty extremely thin people within its narrow bead board-lined walls. Talk about thinking small.

After I navigated through insane parade traffic, I arrived at NOLA Apothecary well past eleven o'clock, fearing that I had missed the show. Then I saw the kid from Tipitina's, Miles Lafayette, going on-stage with his own band, Indie Darling. Wtf? After they played a promising short set, I learned a few things: that the band members of Indie Darling are all students of our local Randolph Academy, where The Vows' guitarist, Noah Seymour, is their teacher. Weird, right? I also learned that The Vows' original bassist, Mike McBride, had unexpectedly passed away a few weeks prior, which was why Pablo Chavez, the band's unofficial fifth member, had a bass guitar around his body.

Any thoughts I might have harbored that The Vows' show was going to disappoint were dispelled immediately, as The Vows opened with a driving, up-tempo rock song that I hadn't heard before. Gary

Davis Gary's voice was both honeyed and husky as ever, pitch-perfect in the song's concluding chorus, "What little we learn we learn a little too late." From there, the band mostly played a heavy dose of their best-selling album, "The Weary Boys," an album I am proud to say that I still listen to today, and often. The first song they resurrected from it, "I Want To Die in San Francisco," with its cacophonous stomp and ringing guitars, sounded as fresh as anything being released these days, a testament to how influential The Vows are to today's younger bands. Later, after an inspired cover version of The Cure's "Just Like Heaven," with the aforementioned Miles Lafayette taking over the vocals, Agnes Waterstown, of the defunct indie band The Autumn Set, appeared on-stage as a backup singer and musician. Wielding one of Seymour's guitars, she led off a desperate, rocking version of Neil Young's "Hey Hey My My (Into the Black)," harmonizing wonderfully with Gary's ironic whispers of the song's lyrics: "Once you're gone you can't come back/The king is gone but he's not forgotten/Is this the story of a Johnny Rotten?/It is better to burn out than it is to fade away/Hey hey, my my, rock and roll can never die." Then came a clearly unrehearsed version of Blondie's "Heart of Glass," with Waterstown calling out the chord changes to the rest of the band while singing flirtatiously, "Once I had a love and it was a gas/Soon found out had a heart of glass/Seemed like the real thing only to find/Mucho mistrust, love's gone behind."

What followed was as welcome as summer rain in New Orleans—a hilarious, four-minute, energetic drum solo from Elliott, during which every band member hurled random objects at him to get him to stop drumming. Next came a trio of The Vows' ethereal dance-inspired hits, delightfully played in the order they are presented on the album: "Dizzy," "Magnolia," and a more up-tempo "Ton of Love," which brought the crowd to near hysterics with Gary Davis Gary pounding on his keyboard like a madman.

The rest of the night's set found the band at its carefree best, as they jumped between playing random covers and more songs from "The Weary Boys." Early on, during an extended version of "She Is So Deep," the band's signature hit, Gary Davis Gary walked through the crowd and offered to share the microphone with any audience member willing to sing the song's chorus along with him. The band also wielded their humor often. At one point near the end of their set, when someone threw an empty bag of Doritos onto the stage, Gary announced to the crowd, "I'd hit that." Or after a particularly sloppy guitar solo from Seymour, bassist Chavez told Seymour to turn off his "suck button." Gary Davis Gary's last words to the crowd were, "We don't have a mailing list because we are terminal."

During their only encore, a slowed-down alt-country version of Dylan's "Tangled Up in Blue," in which Miles Lafayette appeared onstage, once again, to play rhythm guitar with the band, guitarist Seymour and vocalist Waterstown (I had always heard rumors) started kissing passionately during the song's middle, much to everyone's applause. It was the perfect song to conclude a perfect evening. Suffice it to say that The Vows never sounded better, nor appeared looser. But was their show a one-time thing, or will they continue to make more music?

I, at least, know my recommendation.

Hey, hey, my, my. Rock and roll can never die.

Travis Ian Smith is the author of *The Salt Flowers*,
a collection of poetry published in 2010 by MT Pages.
He lives in New Orleans, where he teaches literature,
film, and writing in the School of Continuing Studies
at Tulane University.
Indie Darling is his first novel.

CPSIA information can be obtained at www.ICGtesting.com
Printed in the USA
LVOW07s1747040516

486686LV00001B/70/P